PUFFIN BOOKS

AQUILA 2

drew Norriss was born in Scotland, went to
ersity in Ireland and taught history in a sixth-form
ege in England for ten years before becoming a
-time writer. In the course of twenty years, he has
ten and co-written some hundred and fifty
odes of situation comedies and children's drama
television. He has also written many books for
dren, including *Aquila*, which won the Whitbread
ldren's Book of the Year in 1997, and *The Unluck-
Boy in the World*, which won the Lancashire Schools
tastic Book Prize in 2007.

or more information about Andrew's books, go to
rewnorriss.co.uk.

rriss has a wonderful light comic touch'
Sunday Telegraph

'Andrew Norriss keeps the reader hooked through
narrative that is both comic and touching'
writeaway.org.uk on *The Unluckiest Boy in the World*

D0278868

1804231766

Books by Andrew Norriss

AQUILA
AQUILA 2
BERNARD'S WATCH
CTRL-Z
MATT'S MILLION
THE PORTAL
THE TOUCHSTONE
THE UNLUCKIEST BOY IN THE WORLD

ANDREW NORRISS

AQUILA 2

WK
4/4.

PUFFIN

PUFFIN BOOKS

Published by the Penguin Group
Penguin Books Ltd, 80 Strand, London WC2R ORL, England
Penguin Group (USA) Inc., 375 Hudson Street, New York, New York 10014, USA
Penguin Group (Canada), 90 Eglinton Avenue East, Suite 700, Toronto, Ontario, Canada M4P 2Y3
(a division of Pearson Penguin Canada Inc.)
Penguin Ireland, 25 St Stephen's Green, Dublin 2, Ireland (a division of Penguin Books Ltd)
Penguin Group (Australia), 250 Camberwell Road, Camberwell, Victoria 3124, Australia
(a division of Pearson Australia Group Pty Ltd)
Penguin Books India Pvt Ltd, 11 Community Centre, Panchsheel Park, New Delhi – 110 017, India
Penguin Group (NZ), 67 Apollo Drive, Rosedale, North Shore 0632, New Zealand
(a division of Pearson New Zealand Ltd)
Penguin Books (South Africa) (Pty) Ltd, 24 Sturdee Avenue, Rosebank,
Johannesburg 2196, South Africa

Penguin Books Ltd, Registered Offices: 80 Strand, London WC2R ORL, England

puffinbooks.com

First published 2010
002

Copyright © Andrew Norriss, 2010
All rights reserved

The moral right of the author has been asserted

Set in Plantin 12/15.85pt
Typeset by Palimpsest Book Production Limited, Grangemouth, Stirlingshire
Printed in Great Britain by Clays Ltd, St Ives plc

British Library Cataloguing in Publication Data
A CIP catalogue record for this book is available from the British Library

ISBN: 978-0-141-32853-9

www.greenpenguin.co.uk

MIX
Paper from
responsible sources
FSC
www.fsc.org   FSC™ C018179

Penguin Books is committed to a sustainable
future for our business, our readers and our planet.
This book is made from Forest Stewardship
Council™ certified paper.

ALWAYS LEARNING   **PEARSON**

For Helen, Steve and Megan
– a whole family of eagles

CHAPTER ONE

New York was very big.

Tom and Geoff had known that before they got there, of course, but even so when you actually saw it – when you were floating in the air three hundred feet above the waters of the Hudson, with the island of Manhattan directly in front of you, every part of it sprouting buildings of an impossible size – it still took your breath away.

For several seconds, neither of them spoke.

'Well . . .' Geoff was the first to recover his voice. 'We did it!' He turned to his friend and grinned. 'Well, *you* did!'

Tom was the one who had done the navigating and he was, though he did not say so, rather pleased with himself. In the weeks since he and Geoff had first discovered Aquila, in a cave back in England, they had flown it over half a dozen countries, but crossing the Atlantic had been different. Flying over land, you had roads and rivers to help guide you to where you wanted to go, but crossing an ocean, there was nothing beneath you but three thousand miles of water.

Tom had worked out how to do it though. He had found out about lines of longitude and latitude, learned about the minutes, degrees and seconds of co-ordinates, given the right ones to Aquila and now . . . now here they were, floating in the air alongside the raised arm of the Statue of Liberty.

That was quite big as well.

'Have we got time to take a look around?' asked Geoff.

Tom looked at his watch. The flight that afternoon was only supposed to be a test run, and he had promised his mother he'd be home by four . . . but it was only two thirty, so they had half an hour in hand.

'Fifteen minutes,' he said. 'But after that, we need to go straight back, OK?'

'OK!' His hands lightly on the controls, Geoff took them down over Ellis Island and towards the city. If anyone had seen them, they might have been surprised to see an object about the shape and size of a small power boat floating through the air with no visible means of support – but nobody did see them, of course. Tom had already double-checked that the yellow light that made Aquila invisible was turned on.

Geoff took them neatly across the water and into one of the vast glass and concrete canyons of Manhattan. Flying down a six-lane thoroughfare, a few metres above the traffic, the buildings rearing up on either side of them looked even bigger.

'If you want Central Park,' said Tom, looking up from the map he had brought, 'it's straight ahead.'

But New York was far too exciting to steer anywhere in a straight line. Although it was Sunday, the main streets were teeming with people and Geoff flew them randomly up one road and down another, past theatres and cinemas, past outdoor markets and museums, past shops selling more things than anyone could possibly want, past cafes with tables and chairs set out on the pavement . . .

And then Geoff decided he wanted Tom to take a photo. He always got Tom to take a photo when they went somewhere new, to put up on the wall when they got home.

'We don't really have time –' Tom tried to say, but Geoff was not listening. He had turned Aquila to the right, brought it down to a spot just in front of the pavement and was already climbing out.

Only one person seemed to notice – an elderly man in a dark suit – and you could see the startled look on his face as, from his point of view, a boy appeared to step out of thin air and cross the pavement in front of him. But as Geoff took up his position in front of the imposing doorway of a department store, you could see the man deciding he must have imagined it. After all, people don't suddenly appear out of nowhere, and the man shook his head and moved on. Tom could never quite believe it, but that was how it happened every time.

He took out his mobile and was so busy taking Geoff's picture that he didn't see the taxi until it was almost too late. The yellow cab was heading straight for him and, as Aquila was invisible, the driver had no idea he was there. It was only at the last second that Tom reached out and banged his thumb on to the up button.

Aquila was controlled by four buttons, arranged like the petals of a flower between the handlebars that steered it. One sent you up, one down and the other two took you forward and back. The harder you pushed them, the faster you went and, although Tom had his thumb on the button for less than a second, by the time he released it, he was several thousand feet up in the air.

It was better than the taxi crashing into him though. The impact would not have hurt Aquila – you could drive Aquila through a brick wall without scratching it, as Tom had proved on more than one occasion – but the collision would have been disastrous for the taxi and its driver.

His heart pounding in his chest, Tom pushed the down button, a little more carefully this time, and gently descended between the vast buildings until he came to a halt a few metres above the ground.

That was when he realized, as he looked around, that there were hardly any people, that there were no shops or cafes and that the buildings on either side were mostly houses and hotels. He thought he had gone straight up and then straight back down again, but this was clearly not what had happened. Looking around, he could see he was no longer in the same street.

Tom tried not to panic. He began by flying Aquila backwards and forwards in case the place where he had left Geoff was somewhere further up or down the street, but there was no sign of him. Then he tried hopping over the buildings to the streets on either side to see if one of them was familiar, but there was still nothing he could recognize.

Then he panicked.

He knew what had happened. Or thought he did. In the rush to avoid hitting the taxi, he must have touched either the forward or the back button at the same time as the up – or maybe his arm had brushed against the handlebars that swung Aquila's nose to the right or left – it didn't matter. What mattered was that, instead of going directly up, Aquila had gone forward or side-ways as well. So that when he came down he had landed in a different street and with no idea how far he might have travelled or in which direction.

This was not good.

It was not good because, somewhere in New York, his friend Geoff was standing on the pavement, wait-ing for him – and Tom had no idea how to find him. They hadn't bothered to notice which streets they had been moving along as they cruised around the city. Looking at the people and the sights had been much more interesting and now, ten minutes after he had shot up into the air to avoid the taxi, Tom tried desperately to think what he should do.

If he didn't find Geoff, the whole Aquila adventure would be over. If he wasn't home by four o'clock, then his mother would ring Geoff's parents to ask where he was, Geoff's parents would say they thought the boys had gone to the park to play football, Tom's mother would call the police and then . . .

And then the truth would come out.

From the first day they had found Aquila – before they knew what it was or even much of what it could do – the boys had known that, if they wanted to keep it, they would need to keep their extraordinary discovery a secret. That, they had agreed, would have to be Rule Number One. No one else must know about it. Because if they did, the one thing you could be sure of was that they would not allow Aquila to stay in the hands of two twelve-year-old boys.

He needed to do something and to do it quickly, Tom thought, but doing things quickly had never been his strong suit. If only New York wasn't so big . . . If only he had some clue where Geoff was . . . If only there was someone who could give him directions and . . .

And then he remembered that there was one person who might be able to do exactly that.

Well, not a person exactly . . .

In front of him in Aquila, along what would be the dashboard if he were sitting in a car, stretched a row of coloured lights. Tom reached forward and pressed a small green light over to the left. The words 'HI!

WHAT CAN I DO FOR YOU?' appeared in the air in front of him.

Aquila could speak in nearly twenty-eight thousand languages – though perhaps 'speaking' was not strictly accurate. Its vocal generator had been destroyed some six thousand years before, but it could still communicate with words.

'I'm looking for Geoff,' said Tom, 'and I need to get back to where I left him. Do you remember where that was?'

'OH, YES.' The words flashed up in the air. 'I REMEMBER IT WELL.' And then, above the words, there appeared a picture of Geoff, standing outside the department store.

Tom felt a surge of relief. 'And could you take me there?'

'I COULD.'

There was a pause, before Tom remembered that Aquila only actually did anything when you gave it a specific instruction.

'I want you to take me back there now,' he said. 'OK?'

Aquila was rising through the air even before he had finished speaking and, when it was above the surrounding buildings, its nose swung round to the right, it moved forward a hundred metres or so and then it descended again to the level of the road. On the pavement in front of him, Tom could see a rather worried-looking Geoff peering anxiously up and down.

'Geoff!' Tom hissed, trying to speak so that only his friend would hear. 'Straight in front of you!' And he put out the stick.

When you're climbing into something invisible, it helps to know where it is, and that was why they had worked out the system with the stick. As soon as Geoff saw it, he walked directly across the pavement, swung himself into Aquila and pulled the stick in after him.

'Where on earth have you been?' he demanded. 'I've been standing there for ages. I thought you'd had an accident or something.'

'I did sort of,' said Tom. 'Sorry.' He moved Aquila quickly upwards so that another taxi didn't run into the back of him. 'I got lost.' He reached out and banged the blue button on the far left. It was the one that told Aquila to take them back to Stavely as quickly as possible and, a split second later, Aquila shot up into the sky, turned east and headed towards England.

On the flight home Tom explained what had happened – the lurching into the air to avoid the taxi, the finding himself in the wrong street, the panic as he realized he had no idea where Geoff was – and how he had eventually found his way back by asking Aquila.

'What we need,' said Geoff thoughtfully, when Tom had finished his story, 'is for me to get a mobile. That way, if one of us gets lost or anything, he can call the other one and find out where they are.'

Tom had had a mobile since he was six, but Geoff's parents had always resisted the idea. They had told him, on more than one occasion, that if he wanted one, he could save up and buy it himself.

Tom agreed that Geoff getting a phone would be an excellent idea. There had been several occasions in the last few weeks when it would have been useful.

'But you'd need to get one of the ones that work anywhere in the world,' he added. 'And I would as well.' He paused. 'I think they cost a lot more than ordinary phones.'

Forty minutes later they were still discussing how expensive a mobile that worked in Europe and America as well as England might be, and where they might get the money to buy one, as Aquila began to descend and, soon after, parked itself neatly in the room at the top of the old water tower in Stavely. It was three minutes to four, and outside it was raining.

'I'll fly you home,' said Geoff. 'You don't want to walk in that.'

He took the controls and steered Aquila out of the window, over the treetops, and flew them down to the southern end of town where Tom lived. In less than a minute, they were hovering outside Tom's house, where there was a large, expensive-looking car parked in the driveway.

'Looks like you've got visitors,' said Geoff as he manoeuvred Aquila under the porch so that Tom could climb out without getting wet. 'I'll leave you to find out about the phones, shall I? And I'll think how we can get the money.'

'OK,' Tom agreed, and he waited as Geoff flew off.

Although Aquila was invisible, if you looked carefully, there was a sort of bubble in the rain that told you where it was. It was an interesting effect.

He was reaching into his pocket for his key when the front door opened and his mother appeared.

'I thought I heard you,' said Mrs Baxter. 'Come along, I want you to . . .' She stopped, staring at his clothes. 'Have you just arrived?'

'Yes,' said Tom. 'Why?'

'You're all dry.' Mrs Baxter's face wrinkled in puzzlement. 'How did you walk through the rain without getting wet?'

'Geoff was with me,' said Tom. 'He has an umbrella.'

'Oh.' Mrs Baxter peered out at the driving rain and then back at Tom. If she had been in a different mood, she might have asked why even his shoes were completely dry, but at the moment there were more important things on her mind.

'Come along,' she said. 'There's someone I want you to meet.'

She led the way through the hall to the sitting room, where a cake and some tea things had been set out on the table and a short, broad-shouldered man in a blue suit was sitting in an armchair.

'This is Alan,' said Mrs Baxter. 'We were at school together. Alan? This is my son, Tom.'

'Hi, Tom.' The man called Alan stood up and extended his hand in greeting. 'Good to meet you.'

And, sometimes, that is how the really big adventures in life begin. Not with getting lost in New York, or travelling across the Atlantic at speeds of more than a mile a second, but with a man in a suit standing in your sitting room holding out his hand and saying, 'Hi.'

CHAPTER TWO

'You don't *know* that he's a boyfriend,' said Geoff the next morning as they were flying to school. 'I mean you didn't see them kissing or anything, did you?'

'They didn't have to be.' Tom winced slightly as Geoff brought them down over the rooftops, missing a chimney pot by millimetres. 'I could tell as soon as I saw him.'

For as long as he could remember, Tom and his mother had lived alone in their house in Gilmore Road. His father had left when Tom was three, and there had never been anyone else. Mrs Baxter had suffered for some years from an illness called agoraphobia, which meant she was frightened of going outdoors. So she had never met anyone new and only rarely invited anyone into the house.

Recently, however, things had changed. Tom's mother had got better, she had started going out and now she had met a man. Tom could already imagine what would happen next. In a few months, she and Alan would probably get married, soon after that he would start telling Tom what he could and couldn't do, there would be arguments and quarrelling, and the quiet, peaceful life he had known for so long would be gone forever.

'You're doing it again!' said Geoff.

He raced over the grass and brought Aquila to a dead halt just behind the domestic-science block. It was the sort of stop that should have sent both boys straight out over the bonnet, but for some reason that never happened in Aquila. However fast you accelerated or decelerated, inside the lifepod you didn't feel the change of speed at all.

'Doing what?'

'Worrying.' Geoff floated them down to just above the tarmac. 'When there's no reason.' He picked up his bag, climbed out of Aquila then began rummaging through his pocket for the dog whistle.

'But there *is* a reason.' Tom climbed out of the other side. 'I told you. As soon as I saw him, I knew . . .'

'You don't *know* anything,' said Geoff firmly.

He found the whistle and blew four short blasts. It was the signal that would send Aquila thirty feet up into the air, where it would wait for them until they called it back down. They could have used an ordinary whistle, or simply told Aquila where to go, but the dog whistle had the advantage that nobody – apart from dogs – could hear it. It helped not to draw attention to where they were and what they were doing.

'Look.' Geoff slung his bag over his shoulder. 'Your mum had tea with someone she knew from school, that's all. It's not something you have to panic about. It's what normal people do all the time.'

Tom had to admit that Geoff could be right. He did tend to worry about things that might happen and often never did. And if Geoff *was* right, and his mother had simply been having tea with a friend . . .

It was a consoling thought, and he found, as he followed Geoff into school, that he was feeling a lot better.

At lunchtime, the boys went to see Miss Taylor. The Deputy Head saw them in her office every Monday at one o'clock so that she could talk about any problems they might be having with their work. For most of their school careers, Tom and Geoff had carefully avoided doing any work, let alone talking about it to anyone, but that was something else that had changed in the weeks since they had found Aquila.

'Mr Urquart tells me you wanted him to explain about lines of longitude and latitude last week,' said Miss Taylor, looking up from her notebook at the boys on the other side of her desk. 'And that you wanted to know how people navigated using geographical co-ordinates.' She peered over the top of her glasses. 'Planning a trip abroad, are we?'

'We're just . . . interested in geography,' said Tom.

'Very interested,' added Geoff.

Miss Taylor leaned back in her chair. 'And this morning,' she went on, 'Miss Poulson says you were asking her about how you change pounds into dollars, and where to find out about exchange rates . . .'

'We're interested in those too,' said Geoff.

'Very interested,' added Tom.

'You've also been asking Mr Bampford –' Miss Taylor consulted her notebook again – 'about satellite phones.' She held up a hand before either of the boys could answer. 'Yes, I know. Don't tell me. You were interested . . .'

Unfortunately, this was what happened when you had a machine like Aquila. There were so many things you needed to find out and, when you asked people, they thought it meant you were interested, and wanted to learn. Miss Taylor had been so impressed by the number of things the boys wanted to find out about that she had organized a whole timetable of extra lessons for them. She said that anyone that hungry for knowledge deserved all the help they could get and, after years spent sitting at the back of the class doing their best not to be noticed, it had all come as something of a shock.

The extra lessons might not have been what the boys wanted, but the results had not been as disastrous as they had feared. Geoff, for instance, after eight years of school, was actually learning to read, while Tom was making the sort of progress that might one day allow him to pass the exams that would let him fulfil his dream of becoming a geologist.

'It's all right,' said Miss Taylor, 'I'm not complaining. Quite the reverse. And I have some good reports here from the staff about your work.' She tapped at a file on her desk. 'Miss Stevenson says your reading progress, Geoff, is excellent and Mr Duncan –' Miss Taylor shifted her gaze to Tom – 'says that your maths is little short of astonishing. He tells me you mastered multiplying numbers in brackets after just one lesson!' She smiled approvingly.

'Well done! That's all I can say, really. Both of you. *Very* well done!'

Monday was always a long school day. There was double maths in the morning, double English in the afternoon and then, while everyone else went home, Geoff had an extra reading lesson with Miss Stevenson and Tom had extra science with Mr Bampford. So it was quite a relief, at four thirty, to walk round to the domestic-science block, blow three short blasts and two long on the whistle to bring down Aquila, climb inside and fly back to the Eyrie for what was undoubtedly the best part of the day.

In the first two weeks after they had brought Aquila back from the cave where they had found it, they had kept it in the garage at Tom's house. They had had to move it, though, when Tom's mother recovered from her agoraphobia, and the search for somewhere safe to keep it – somewhere no one ever went or would ever find it – had not been easy. When Geoff discovered the water tower, however, both boys had known at once it was the perfect solution.

The tower had been built more than a century before on a hill in the woods to the east of Stavely, to provide water for the new houses being put up on that side of the town. It had been abandoned for more than thirty years now but, instead of pulling it down, the council had simply boarded up the door at the bottom, surrounded the base with barbed wire and left it there.

When the boys first flew through the empty window space at the top, they had found a room, about five metres square, where they could leave Aquila in perfect safety. When they had finished with it for the day, they blew a signal on a dog whistle of two long blasts and two short, and Aquila would fly itself fifty metres into the air and park inside. When they wanted it to come down again, they blew three short blasts and two long and Aquila would arrive invisibly to the right of whoever had blown the whistle.

They called it the Eyrie because Aquila – the name painted in gold on the front of the lifepod – was the Latin word for an eagle and an eyrie is an eagle's nest. Eagles build their eyries high up on a cliff face or at the top of a tree, where no one else can reach them – and it described the room at the top of the tower rather well.

Over the weeks, it had become a very comfortable place to hang out. Mrs Murphy, the old lady who lived next door to Tom, had let them have odd bits of furniture from her attic, so there was a table and chairs, an old sofa and a square of carpet on the floor. There were shelves along the back walls where the boys kept mementos of their trips abroad and a board where Geoff pinned his photos. They had found a fridge and a television at the Stavely Recycling Centre, Aquila provided the power that ran them and, best of all, the place was completely private.

No one ever disturbed them in the Eyrie because, quite apart from the fact they were fifty metres up in the air, nobody knew they were there. Tom's mother thought he was round with Geoff – which in a way he was – and Geoff's parents presumed that he was with Tom.

So, at the end of a school day, the boys would fly back to the water tower and grab a cold drink from the fridge. Tom would produce the slices of cake that his mother always gave him in case he got hungry during the day, and they would sit on the sofa, the looming bulk of Aquila floating silently beside them, and stare contentedly out at the town.

'I've been thinking,' said Geoff, 'about how we could use Aquila to get enough money to buy a mobile.'

'And?'

'And I can't think of anything. Well, nothing we could use.'

It was distinctly frustrating. There were a million ways you could use Aquila to make money – like offering to fly people to New York for a fraction of the cost and in a fraction of the time for a start – but doing anything like that meant telling people about Aquila, and that was the problem. Because telling anyone about

Aquila was the one thing they had to avoid. It was Rule Number One. If they wanted to keep it, no one else must know about it. Ever.

Geoff had briefly considered the idea of using Aquila to steal the money they wanted – when you have an invisible machine, with a laser that can cut through steel and stone like butter, robbing a bank would be simple enough – but somehow that solution seemed a little extreme. Quite apart from what his parents would say if they found out.

'Is a phone going to be very expensive?' he asked.

'The sort we need would cost about a hundred pounds,' Tom told him. He had quizzed Mr Bampford very carefully on the subject. 'And we'd need two of them.' He added that the science teacher had also said he thought you needed to be over eighteen before you could sign a contract to buy one, so it looked like the phones were going to be one of those nice ideas that would never actually happen. The conversation turned instead to what they might do at the weekend.

The weekend was when the boys had time to go on proper flights to somewhere interesting and they took it in turns to decide where they might go. Tom's hobby was geology, so he usually wanted to visit somewhere he could collect rocks. At the moment, he was particularly keen on adding to his collection of mountain peaks. On the shelves at the back of the Eyrie, he already had small sections sliced with Aquila's laser from the top of the Matterhorn, Mont Blanc and the four highest peaks in Britain. The Pico del Aneto, the highest mountain in the Pyrenees, was next on his list.

Geoff wanted to go back to New York, particularly now they knew how easy it was to get there, but he was also keen on a trip to the beach. Not in England, where the weather had been grey and damp for weeks, but somewhere warm and sunny – the south of France perhaps – and they were still discussing the possibilities when it was time to go home.

Later that evening, up in his bedroom, Tom was writing up the events of the weekend in an exercise book. He kept a careful note of most of the things they did in Aquila – particularly when they discovered anything new that it could do, like being able to retrace its steps and go back to where it had been. And he was busily writing when his mother came in with a mug of hot chocolate and clean clothes for school the following day.

'I've just had a phone call from Alan,' she said, placing the mug of chocolate on Tom's desk. 'He's offered to take us out to lunch next Sunday.'

'I'm going round to Geoff's on Sunday,' said Tom.

'Tell him you're busy,' said his mother. 'I'm sure he won't mind.' She placed the clothes on the chair by Tom's bed, careful not to disturb the creases she had ironed into his trousers. 'Alan wants to take us to the Royal Oak! That'll be a treat, eh?' She ruffled her son's hair and looked briefly at the exercise book open in front of him. 'Still writing your stories, are you? Don't stay up too late!'

As she left the room, Tom sighed. If Geoff were here, he would probably say that his mother going out for lunch with Alan didn't mean anything – it was just something that normal people did all the time – but Tom found it difficult to believe that was true.

Life had been a lot simpler in the days when his mother stayed home all day and never met anyone, he thought, and a tiny part of him couldn't help wishing she still had agoraphobia.

CHAPTER THREE

When Tom and Geoff first found Aquila, they had very quickly discovered what it could do. Or thought they had. Geoff had pressed one of the purple lights on the control column to see what happened, and they had suddenly found themselves two thousand feet up in the air. Aquila could fly. It was only slowly that they had come to realize that it could do a lot of other things as well and, even now, Tom reckoned, they had barely scratched the surface of its capabilities.

They had found out some things though. They knew – because Aquila had told them – that it was the lifepod from a Denebian battlecruiser that had come through a portal some six thousand years before and been ambushed by a flotilla of Yrrillian warships. Tom had read Aquila's account of the battle – and seen pictures of how the cruiser had been sliced open and the crew had scrambled to the lifepods in their efforts to escape. Aquila was one of the lifepods and had made its way to Earth. But knowing all of that left you, if anything, with even more questions than when you started.

Like who were the Denebians? Why had their ship been ambushed? And what was a portal? The trouble was that there were so many questions you could ask, and each time you got the answer to one of them, it led you to several more.

That was why Geoff had suggested that, in the short term at least, they concentrate on finding out what Aquila could do, rather than investigating where it came from or what had happened to it in the past. Gesturing to the row of coloured lights along the dash on that first day in the Eyrie, he had suggested that, for a start, they should find out what happened when you pressed each one of them.

It sounded like a sensible plan, and the boys had sat in Aquila while Geoff pointed to each of the lights and asked what it did. The reply would flash up in the air in front of them and Tom would read it out so that Geoff, whose reading was still a little uncertain, would know what it said as well. The answers, however, were not always as simple as the question.

A few buttons were easy enough. There was the large yellow button that made Aquila invisible – no complications there. There was the button that fired the laser – which started eleven fires the first time they tried it, but which they now used mostly to heat up beans or make toast. And there was the button which, when you pressed it, flew Aquila to the outskirts of a town in Bulgaria.

But with many of the lights, when you asked Aquila what they did, the answer was so complicated you could spend hours trying to work out what it meant. When Aquila said that pressing the little purple light on the left activated the temporal stasis generator, you could sit and read through thousands of words – as Tom did – and still not have much idea what it was really for. He knew it froze people into a sort of bubble outside time because they had accidentally used it on old Mrs Murphy next door, but *why* you would want to do it was still a mystery.

And then they had discovered that the lights were only the start of what Aquila could do. They were, Tom discovered one afternoon, simply the controls for the things you wanted Aquila to do the most often. They were like the short cuts you could put on a computer, so that instead of having to give it detailed instructions every time, you simply pressed one key.

Each of the lights that ran along the dash in front of the seat in Aquila could in fact be set to do something quite different. Tom had reset the button that took you to Bulgaria, for instance, so that it now flew Aquila back to the water tower – something that had been very useful on the odd occasion when they had got lost. You could set any of the lights for any of the things that Aquila could do – and Aquila could do a lot of things.

A *lot* of things.

24

The lifepod had been designed to keep a Denebian alive in the deep reaches of space, carry it to the nearest habitable planet and then keep it safe until it was rescued. It was crammed with everything the makers could think of that might be useful in doing that. When Tom had once asked it to list all its functions, he had spent the next half an hour watching titles scrolling up through the air in front of him. That was when he paused the process and asked how long it was going to take, and Aquila told him that viewing a complete list of things it could do would take approximately three and a half days.

Just to look at the titles.

Since they were never going to be able to work their way through the whole list, Geoff had suggested that maybe they should work things the other way round. Instead of trying to find out what Aquila *could* do, they should carry on using it the way they had and only ask it something when they needed help.

That was how Tom had worked out how to navigate to New York, that was how they had worked out how to carry a sofa to the top of the Eyrie and that was why Tom decided to ask Aquila if it could set up an early warning system so that taxis didn't run into the back of him.

The incident in New York was not the first time the boys had narrowly avoided an accident. They usually flew high enough to miss cars crashing into them, but they had once been hit by a particularly tall lorry, birds regularly knocked themselves out on the hull and, most worrying of all, they had had two near collisions in the air – one with a Harrier GR7 and one with a passenger jet on a descent path near Luton.

The trouble was that, though Aquila was invisible, it was still there, and it was protected by a force field that could withstand collision with anything up to and including a nuclear explosion. If either of the planes had hit them, or the taxi, the damage would have been a lot worse than a stunned bird or the roof ripped off the top of a lorry.

So on Saturday morning, while Geoff was at his reading lesson with Miss Stevenson, Tom asked Aquila if there was some way it could warn him of anything coming near, and perhaps do something to make sure whatever it was didn't hit them.

Aquila assured him that it could, and Tom instructed it to attach the alarm to an orange light on the dash that had previously switched on the meson fluctuator – one of several buttons that didn't seem to do anything they'd found useful. The result was, in many ways, a typical example of how asking Aquila to do something could sometimes get so complicated that you wished by the end that you hadn't bothered.

When Geoff arrived at the Eyrie, soon after twelve, Tom told him what he had done and Geoff was suitably impressed.

'Nice move,' he said, nodding approvingly. 'And all I have to do is press this button, right?'

'You press the button,' Tom told him, 'and Aquila

warns you if anything's coming too close, and then makes sure it doesn't crash into you.'

'Cool!' Geoff reached forward and pressed his finger on the button.

Instantly, the air in front of him was filled with flashing red lights and huge letters in the air that spelled out 'DANGER! DANGER! ALERT! ALERT!'. At the same time, Aquila vibrated, violently, in time to the flashing lights.

Startled, the boys looked round, up, down and sideways to see what might be coming towards them when they had thought they were safe in the Eyrie. They couldn't see anything though, and when Tom eventually turned off the alarm and asked Aquila what the danger was, it turned out a fly had flown in through the window.

It took Tom a while to make the adjustments. He told Aquila that an object as small as a fly was not what he had meant and that the warning alarm did not need to include so many lights and the heavy vibrations. Aquila asked what changes he wanted and they decided in the end that only an object more than a metre in width should set off the alarm – and then it should simply be the orange light flashing on the dash.

They did a test run of the new settings on a small road to the north of Stavely. Geoff brought Aquila down to road level at a point where they were facing the oncoming traffic and could easily see if a car was coming. That way, he said, if Aquila's warning system didn't work, they would have time to get out of the way.

The warning system worked perfectly. After a minute or so, the orange light started flashing and a moment later, a car came round the corner towards them. Geoff was just moving his thumb to the up button so that the car could pass underneath when, instead of turning the corner, it veered off the road, careering fifty metres into a field of wheat, trailing fence posts and barbed wire, before finally coming to a halt.

'Why did it do that?' said Tom, a little nervously.

'No idea,' said Geoff. 'Better go and see if they're all right though.'

He flew them up and over the field until they were floating alongside the car. There was only one person inside, a woman, slumped unconscious in the driver's seat.

As Geoff reached inside the open window to turn off the engine, Tom remembered that, as well as giving a warning, he had asked Aquila to make sure that a collision didn't happen. And the lifepod, he remembered, could be very precise . . .

He pressed his hand on the small green button and, even before the words 'HI, WHAT CAN I DO FOR YOU?' had appeared in front of him, asked, 'What happened to the car?'

'VEHICLE WAS DIVERTED TO AVOID COLLISION AS INSTRUCTED.'

'What's it saying?' asked Geoff, peering at the letters.

'It's saying it made the car crash, so that it wouldn't bump into us,' said Tom. 'Is she all right?'

He was talking to Geoff, but it was Aquila that answered.

'SUBJECT HAS BEEN RENDERED UNCON-SCIOUS, BUT WILL RECOVER FULL FUNC-TIONALITY IN FOURTEEN MINUTES.'

Tom's mobile was back at the Eyrie, but they found the woman had one of her own in the car and used it to call an ambulance. Then they waited until it arrived, along with three police cars, and watched as the woman was carefully taken out and put on a stretcher. Her eyes opened as she was being lifted into the ambulance and she seemed OK as she tried to ask what had happened.

'I'll have another go with the instructions,' said Tom as they watched the ambulance drive away. 'So it doesn't do anything like that again.'

'Or perhaps we should just skip the alarm,' said Geoff, 'and go back to keeping a good lookout.'

And Tom agreed, as they went back to the Eyrie for lunch before heading off to the Pyrenees and the Pico del Ancto, that that might be best.

On Sunday, Tom and his mother had their lunch out with Alan. The Royal Oak was the most expensive hotel in Stavely and lunch there ought to have been a treat. Tom, however, did not enjoy it. There was some-thing about the size of the hotel dining room, the number of knives and forks at each place setting and the exaggerated politeness of the waiters that was a little overpowering.

And, if he were honest, Alan was a bit overpowering as well.

Mrs Baxter's old school friend, with his broad chest and muscled physique, gave the impression that he had never been overpowered by anything or anyone. He was polite, made sure Tom had whatever he wanted to eat and didn't get upset when he knocked over a glass of cola, but Tom couldn't help thinking how much he would have preferred to be out with Geoff in Aquila. His friend had called in that morning to say that he was going off to find a beach in France and have a swim.

'The weather report says it's quite sunny there at the moment,' Geoff had said, sitting in the lifepod as it hovered outside Tom's bedroom window. 'Can I borrow a towel?'

In England, it had been the wettest June for nearly a century and Tom would have liked very much to go to the beach. He went and got a towel and passed it out through the window.

'Thanks!' Geoff stowed it under his seat and put on a pair of sunglasses. 'When do you think you'll be back from this lunch?'

'About two o'clock,' said Tom. His mother had warned him that lunch at the hotel would take at least a couple of hours.

'OK, I'll see you then.' Aquila blinked out of visibility, and Geoff's voice could be heard as he flew off. 'Have a good time!'

In fact, at two o'clock, Tom was still sitting in the

hotel lounge while his mother and Alan had coffee and talked about the party Mrs Baxter was planning.

The party was to celebrate her recovery from agoraphobia and, as far as Tom could tell, she planned to invite more or less everyone she had ever known. She had sent out invitations to relatives, neighbours, friends from work and had even contacted people she'd been to school with, through a website. It was on the website that she had found Alan.

The party was only two weeks away now and Mrs Baxter was full of plans for how she was going to organize the food, what she might do if it rained, who had said they could come and who couldn't, and it was while she was on this subject that she mentioned the name Freddie Dimble.

'Do you remember him?' she asked Alan. 'Only I had an email from him this morning.'

Alan considered this. 'Little fellow with sticky-out ears?' he asked. 'Yes, I do. Didn't he have a crush on you?'

'Oh, I don't remember that!' Mrs Baxter blushed. 'But do you think we should ask him?'

'Why not!' Alan turned to Tom and smiled. 'Half the class had a crush on your mother in those days,' he said. 'And who could blame them!'

Tom managed a vague smile in reply, but inside there was a sinking feeling in his stomach.

'*Do you think we should ask him?*' That was what his mother had said. Not '*Do you think I should ask him?*' but '*Do you think we should . . .*'

31

It didn't sound like the sort of thing you said to someone who was 'just a friend'.

When he finally got home, Tom was up in his room, getting changed into a pair of jeans that didn't have cola spilled down the front of them, when there was a tap on the window.

Opening the window and looking out, there was nothing to be seen, but from somewhere in the emptiness came the sound of Geoff's voice.

'Tom?' he said. 'I think we have a problem.'

'What is it?' asked Tom. 'What's happened?'

'Well . . .' Geoff's voice hesitated. 'There's no one here is there?'

Tom looked quickly around the garden. The trees on either side shielded them from the neighbours and the field at the back was empty. 'All clear,' he said. 'What's wrong?'

Aquila blinked into view and there was no need for Geoff to say anything because Tom could see at once what the problem was.

Geoff was scarlet. The skin on his face, his hands and his arms was a bright, glowing red.

'I think I may have caught the sun a bit,' he said. 'While I was on the beach.'

Tom let out a long sigh. It was definitely a problem. Sunburn, when there had been solid cloud cover in England for the last fortnight, was not going to be easy to explain.

CHAPTER FOUR

Geoff's trip to the beach had started well. After calling at Tom's house to borrow a towel, he had taken Aquila up to a couple of thousand feet, pointed its nose south and headed off for France. A few minutes later he had crossed the Channel, three minutes after that he passed Paris somewhere to his left and, changing course to south-south-east, he had simply kept flying until he got to the Mediterranean.

The sun was shining, the sea was a deep, sparkling blue and he had followed the coastline west for a few miles before coming to what looked like a particularly pleasant sandy beach, where he parked Aquila behind some rocks. He got changed into his swimming things, checked there was no one watching before climbing out, and strolled down to the water.

'It was brilliant,' he told Tom. 'Really brilliant. But then . . .' he hesitated. 'But then I sort of lost track of the time.'

'How long were you there?' Tom asked.

'About two hours, I think.' Geoff had left Aquila outside the window and was standing in Tom's bedroom, studying his reflection in a mirror. 'It wasn't too bad to start with, but flying home it seemed to get worse.' He lifted up his T-shirt. His chest was the same colour as his arms and face, and his whole body radiated heat. 'You think anyone'll notice?'

'Of course they'll notice!' said Tom. 'And they'll want to know how you got like that. What are you going to tell them?'

'I don't know.' Geoff chewed at his bottom lip. 'That's why I came here. I thought you might have an idea.'

'Well, I don't,' said Tom. 'I don't see there's anything you *can* say.'

'Perhaps I could hide in the Eyrie until it's gone.' Geoff patted cautiously at his skin. 'How long would that take?'

'Days,' said Tom. 'And you can't hide anywhere because . . .'

But before he could explain why hiding for several days was not a good solution, the door opened and Mrs Baxter came in.

'If you give me those trousers,' she was saying, 'I'll put them in the wash before . . . Geoff?' She stopped in surprise. 'I didn't know you were here!'

'I let him in,' Tom explained.

'Oh, I see. Well . . .' Mrs Baxter's voice trailed off again as she noticed the colour of Geoff's skin. 'Oh,

34

my goodness! What on earth have you been doing?'

'I . . . I'm not sure,' said Geoff.

Mrs Baxter stepped forward for a closer look. 'That's sunburn!' She frowned. 'How did you get sunburn in this weather?'

Geoff opened his mouth to answer, but no sound came out and it was Tom who had a moment of inspiration.

'I think,' he said, 'Geoff might have been spending too much time under one of those UV lamps.'

'Oh, you haven't!' Mrs Baxter tutted anxiously. 'Didn't your parents tell you how dangerous those things are?'

'No,' said Geoff. 'No, they didn't.'

'Well, they should have,' said Mrs Baxter firmly. 'You're far too young for that sort of thing. How long did you have it on?'

'I'm . . . not sure,' said Geoff.

'Look at the state of you!' Mrs Baxter studied Geoff's arms and neck. 'I'll get you some lotion, but you really must be more careful in future.'

'I will be,' Geoff promised, and when Mrs Baxter had left the room, he turned to Tom. 'What's a UV lamp?'

'They're special lights people use to get a suntan in winter,' he said. 'Mum's got one.'

'So I could tell everyone that's what happened?'

'Well . . .' Tom hesitated. 'It might work.'

'Fantastic!' Geoff sat on the bed and grinned up at his friend. 'I knew one of us would think of something!'

It was, he thought, why he and Tom made such a good team. Whatever happened, one of them always seemed to know how to sort it out.

There was still a bit of the afternoon left after Mrs Baxter had finished putting on the lotion, and the boys took a quick trip down to Salisbury Plain to look at Stonehenge. Geoff did the flying, so that Tom could do his maths homework on the way – with Aquila's help, of course.

Sitting in the lifepod, Tom read out the problems Mr Duncan had set him on ordering negative numbers, and Aquila produced the answers, with the full workings, in the air in front of him. All Tom had to do was copy them out. He felt a brief stab of guilt as he did this – it was cheating after all – but life was so busy at the moment it was the only way he could think of to get everything done.

The homework took no more than ten minutes and, by the time he had finished, they were hovering directly above Stonehenge. There was a crowd of visitors walking round the outside – they were not allowed to get close to the stones themselves – but Tom and Geoff had no such problems.

Geoff flew them down to the outer ring of sarsens, then round in a slow circle before taking them through one of the gaps to the next ring and finally into the centre, where they paused above the stone which Miss Poulson had told them was where a sacrifice was made each year when the sun rose on midsummer's morning. Sitting there, with the rain pattering gently on Aquila's hull, was rather peaceful.

'Are you going to take a chip off one of them,' asked Geoff, 'as a souvenir?'

'I'm not sure,' said Tom. A chunk of one of the stones would be a nice addition to his collection and he had brought his geological hammer but, now that he was here, it didn't seem quite such a good idea.

'They're pretty big,' said Geoff, looking around. 'I don't think anyone's going to notice if a bit goes missing.'

Tom agreed, but decided in the end to leave the stones as they were. Instead, they sat in the lifepod in the centre of the great circle and he told Geoff about lunch at the Royal Oak and spilling cola and Alan and his mother talking about the party. And somehow, surrounded by the stones that had been put there over four thousand years before, none of it seemed to matter quite as much.

That was what Tom had always liked about rocks. Rocks didn't worry about things. They didn't want you to do anything or to make polite conversation, they just . . . *were*. Millions of years might pass, but a rock was still a rock and a stone was still a stone, solid, patient and enduring.

They were the reassuring presence that told you not everything in life has to change.

When Tom tried to hand in his homework to Mr Duncan the next day, he found the maths teacher was not at school.

'He's had to go to the hospital,' said Miss Taylor when the boys reported to her office at lunchtime. 'His wife had a car accident on Saturday. Blacked out and drove straight off the road into a field. They're giving her tests to try to find out what happened.' She took the homework and looked at the pages of neat calculations. 'Did this take you very long? Mr Duncan was worried he might have given you more than you could manage.'

Tom said he'd worked at it on Sunday afternoon, which was true, and Miss Taylor nodded thoughtfully before taking off her glasses and swinging them between her fingers for several seconds before continuing.

'Would you mind,' she said, slowly, 'if I gave you both some advice?'

Tom and Geoff assured her that they wouldn't mind at all.

'It's very good to see you doing all this work,' said Miss Taylor, 'and asking your teachers all these questions about Stonehenge and Norway and how to find out what the weather's like in the Mediterranean, but . . . I'm a little worried that maybe you're pushing too hard.' She held up a hand as if to ward off an interruption. 'Don't get me wrong! Asking questions and being interested in things is all very wonderful, and the last thing I want to do is discourage you, but –' she hesitated – 'perhaps you should remember there are other things in life besides work. It's important to find the right *balance* in life, you know. You need to have a bit of *fun* occasionally as well.'

'You . . . you think we're working too hard?' asked Tom.

'I do.' Miss Taylor nodded.

'And you want us . . . to have more fun?' said Geoff.

'Yes.' Miss Taylor nodded again. 'Having fun is important too, you know.'

Neither of the boys was quite sure what to say.

'My advice would be to throttle back a bit.' The Deputy Head leaned back in her chair. 'Particularly on things like experiments with UV lamps. We don't want you to burn out, do we? Not in any sense of the word. You understand?'

'Wow,' said Geoff when they left the office. 'Miss Taylor telling us not to work too hard. That's a first!'

'Norway . . .' said Tom. 'I haven't been asking any questions about Norway. Have you?'

'I thought it might be a nice place to visit one day,' said Geoff. 'It's got fjords and things, hasn't it?' He set off briskly down the corridor. 'Come on, let's get some lunch. I'm hungry.'

They had lunch in Aquila, sitting in brilliant sunshine at ten thousand feet and, as they ate their sandwiches with miles of dazzling white cloud stretched out beneath them as far as the eye could see, Geoff remarked that it was hard to believe how much life had changed in the last few weeks.

Tom agreed. Life at school was certainly very different from the way it had been even recently. And the odd thing was that, despite all the extra work, despite

39

all the looking things up in books and asking teachers questions, school life was actually a lot more relaxed.

Before, if a teacher had spoken to them at all, it would probably have been to ask why they hadn't handed in some work or to demand, suspiciously, where they were going. These days, however, if Mr Bampford saw them in the corridor, he would stop them to say he had a magazine article on gravity he thought might interest them. Or Miss Poulson would wave them down to say she had a new book on Stonehenge. And when Mr Urquart saw them come into his classroom at break, he would give a little chuckle and ask what it was they were after *this* time . . .

For some reason, all the teachers seemed to *approve* of them, and it was surprising how much difference that approval could make.

At four thirty, they went back to the Eyrie for tea – two large slices of chocolate fudge cake – before flying over to the Stavely recycling centre.

They usually had a look around the recycling centre at least once a week. It was astonishing what people threw away and, one way and another, the centre had provided a lot of comforts for the Eyrie. It was where they had got the colour television, the bookshelves and two of the chairs, and today they were looking for a microwave oven. Tom thought it might be more convenient for heating food than using Aquila's laser – and probably safer. Last time he had tried to reheat a piece of pizza with the laser, he had managed to evaporate not only the food, but the plate it was on and a small section of the table.

The centre closed at four thirty, which meant that when they flew over the locked gates and landed in the parking area, they had the place to themselves. They didn't find a microwave oven but, in one of the bins, Tom found a large oil painting of mountains which he thought would look good on the Eyrie wall, while Geoff found a dartboard and a huge pile of comics. Cheered by their finds, they took them back to the Eyrie before Geoff flew Tom back to his house. Almost the first thing they saw there was Alan's silver Lexus parked in the driveway.

'Looks like your friend's here again,' said Geoff.

'He is not my friend,' said Tom, surprised at how quickly his mood had changed at the sight of the car.

Geoff looked at him. 'You really don't like him, do you?'

'It's not that I don't like him,' said Tom, 'I don't *like* him or *not* like him. I don't know anything about him, do I? He could be a bank robber for all I know.'

Geoff considered this.

'You haven't asked him what he does?'

'No,' said Tom determinedly. 'I don't talk to him if I can help it.'

Tom had decided, as far as possible, to avoid all conversation with Alan. Talking to him might make it look as if he were interested, and Tom wanted it to be quite clear that he was not interested in Alan at all.

'There's other ways of finding out about him without talking to him,' said Geoff. 'If that's what you want.'

'Like what?'

'Well . . .' Geoff ran his fingers lightly over the lights on the dash. 'We have the perfect spying machine here, don't we? If you want to know anything about Alan, all we have to do is follow him. If he does rob banks for a living, it wouldn't take long to find out.'

CHAPTER FIVE

There were two problems with following Alan in Aquila. The first was that, during the week at least, the boys only had a very limited time in which to work. They had about half an hour in the mornings before they went to school, sometimes another half hour at lunchtime, and perhaps an hour or so when school finished – and that was it.

The other problem was finding Alan so that they could follow him. They knew where he lived – Tom had looked it up in his mother's address book – and went round to his house first thing Monday morning, but Alan wasn't there. The house was quite large and modern, set in a nice garden, but there was no sign of Alan, nor of anyone else. Presumably he had already gone to work – wherever that might be. They flew Aquila up and down the front and back of the house, peering in all the windows as they did so, but without learning anything useful.

When they came back to the house at lunchtime and after school, it was the same story. They waited a bit, in case Alan came home, but the place remained firmly deserted. What they really needed, said Geoff, was the address for where he worked.

'Couldn't you ask your mother or something?' he asked.

'I'd rather not,' said Tom. 'Like I said, I don't want her to think I'm interested. I'm sure he'll turn up if we wait long enough.'

And on Thursday lunchtime, Alan did indeed turn up. Hovering in Aquila, the boys watched the Lexus sweep up the drive to the house and Alan dash out and disappear indoors. A few minutes later he came out again in a different shirt, got back into the car and the boys followed him as he drove through Stavely to Tom's house, where Mrs Baxter hurried out of the front door to join him.

They followed the car back into town and watched as Alan parked outside an Italian restaurant off the high street, then took Mrs Baxter by the hand and led her inside. Soon after that, Tom and Geoff had to get back to school for history with Miss Poulson.

'We might find out more at the weekend,' said Tom as Geoff brought Aquila in to land behind the domestic-science block. 'He'll be home then. If we watch him on Saturday and Sunday, that's when we'll see where he goes and things.'

'Watch him on Saturday *and* Sunday?' said Geoff.

'I'm sorry,' said Tom, 'but it's important.' The sight

of his mother and Alan holding hands had made him more determined than ever to find out as much as he could. 'You don't mind, do you?'

'Well . . .' Geoff climbed out of Aquila and blew the four short blasts on the whistle that would send Aquila thirty feet in the air to wait for them. 'If you pushed me, I'd probably admit a slight preference for New York but . . .' He smiled at his friend. 'I guess it'll wait.'

'Thanks,' said Tom. 'It's only for this weekend. Next week you can choose what we do on both days, OK?'

When the weekend came, however, it was not from following him that they learned something new about Alan.

It was Saturday morning, and Tom was up in his room reading in his book about how the blue stones at Stonehenge had been carried from a quarry in Wales, when his mother called him downstairs.

In the hallway, he found Alan with a boy about eight years old. He was small, with short, cropped hair and a large pair of glasses framing big dark eyes that looked unblinkingly up at Tom.

'This is Dunstan,' said Mrs Baxter. 'Alan's son.'

Tom took a moment to absorb that information.

Alan had a son?

'We're going to look after him,' Mrs Baxter went on, 'while Alan deals with an emergency at work.' She reached across and patted Dunstan's head. 'Isn't that right?'

'I'm going out,' said Tom. 'I'm meeting Geoff.'

'Geoff's got a reading lesson until twelve, hasn't he?' said Mrs Baxter. 'That's not for a couple of hours.'

'I'm really sorry about this,' said Alan. 'If it's inconvenient in any way . . .'

'Of course it's not inconvenient!' said Mrs Baxter. 'We're delighted to have him.'

'Well, I'm very grateful.' Alan ran his fingers through his hair and turned to Tom. 'I don't think he'll be any trouble. Usually all you need to do is sit him down in front of a computer.' He turned back to Mrs Baxter. 'I shouldn't be too long. Three hours at the most.'

Fortunately, it turned out Alan was at least right when he said that Dunstan was no trouble to look after. Tom took him upstairs and showed him a computer game he had been given for Christmas that involved attacking a space station, and for the rest of the morning Dunstan swept his way through it with a fierce concentration that gave him maximum points at the first try.

It was as well that he was concentrating on the game because otherwise he might have seen the arm that appeared from out of nowhere outside the window and tapped on the glass soon after midday.

'Dunstan . . .' Tom pressed the pause button. 'Would you go downstairs and ask Mum for a drink?'

'Why?' asked Dunstan.

'Because I'm thirsty.'

Dunstan hesitated a moment, but then got up and walked without a word to the door. As soon as he was gone, Tom went over to the window and opened it.

'Who was that?' Geoff's head appeared, leaning out of the invisible Aquila.

'Dunstan,' said Tom. 'He's Alan's son.'

'He has a son?' Geoff gave a low whistle. 'Does that mean he's –' His head suddenly ducked out of view.

'What sort of drink?'

Dunstan was standing in the doorway.

'What?'

'What sort of drink did you want?' asked Dunstan.

'Water,' said Tom. 'Just . . . water out of the tap.' He waited until he had heard Dunstan going downstairs before telling Geoff that the coast was clear.

'I wondered why you weren't at the Eyrie,' Geoff said. 'Thought I'd come round and see what had happened.' He paused. 'If Alan has a son, does that mean he's married?'

'He used to be,' said Tom. It was the first question he had asked Dunstan himself. 'She died. He's had to leave Dunstan here because he's got an emergency at work.'

'At work?' Geoff nodded thoughtfully. 'Interesting . . .'

'Is it?'

'Well, if you wanted to know what he does for a living,' said Geoff. 'Now's your chance. All we have to do is go and look.'

'I can't go anywhere,' said Tom. 'I've got to look after Dunstan.'

'*You* may have to,' said Geoff, 'but I don't, do I? All

47

I need is an address. If you ask Dunstan where his dad is, I can –'

He blinked out of view again, and Tom turned round to find Dunstan in the doorway with a glass of water.

'Oh, thanks!' Tom walked across the room to collect it. 'Dunstan, do you know where your dad works?'

'Yes,' said Dunstan, and sat back down at the computer.

Asking Dunstan a question, Tom realized, was a bit like talking to Aquila. You had to be quite precise.

'So where does he work? Exactly.'

'On the industrial estate,' said Dunstan. 'Hillside Road. Unit Seventeen.'

The Stavely industrial estate covered an area almost as large as the town itself and consisted of a network of warehouses, small factories and commercial buildings, most of which, as it was Saturday, were deserted and quiet. Geoff found Hillside Road and followed it up a steep hill, past a car-repair firm and a bathroom fitter before finally arriving at Unit 17.

He knew he was in the right place because he could see Alan's Lexus parked in front of the main building. There were several other cars there, but no sign of anyone working and Geoff was debating what to do next when Alan walked briskly out of the main entrance. He was wearing a boiler suit, had a pair of wellingtons on his feet and was pulling on a pair of large rubber gloves as he strode round to the back of the building.

Geoff followed him, a few metres behind, hovering silently in the air, and watched as Alan walked towards a row of tall box-shaped objects, each about the size of a telephone kiosk. There was a long row of them set out on the tarmac and a man with a forklift truck was unloading more from a lorry parked to one side. When Geoff brought Aquila down to where he could look closely, he realized they were lavatories. A long row of portable lavatories.

Three more men, dressed as Alan was in boiler suits and rubber gloves, were busy cleaning the inside of the lavatories that had already been unloaded. One of them had a pressure hose, one was on his hands and knees scrubbing at the floor and the third was attaching the hose from a small tanker to one of the lavatories and turning on a pump.

Alan himself grabbed a bucket and some bleach and set to work.

Well, Geoff thought, they knew what Alan did for a living now.

He cleaned toilets.

'You're quite sure that's what he was doing?' asked Tom. The two boys were sitting on the patio while indoors Dunstan was watching television. They spoke in low voices but Tom had already made sure the volume on the TV was turned up enough for them not to be overheard.

'Positive,' said Geoff for the third time. 'He had the boots, the gloves, the bucket . . .'

Tom sighed. If his mother had to go out with some-one, you could at least hope they managed a football team or spied for the government or something. But if they cleaned toilets . . .

Mrs Baxter put her head out of the kitchen window and called out that lunch was ready if anyone was hungry.

Tom wondered if she knew what Alan did for a living. And, if she did know, did she care?

'We're still not *absolutely* sure there's anything going on between him and your mum,' said Geoff as they moved indoors. 'They could still just be friends . . .'

But you could tell from his voice that he didn't really believe this.

And nor did Tom.

Half an hour later when Alan turned up to collect Dunstan, he was wearing a suit and tie, and smelling faintly of soap. If you hadn't seen him on his hands and knees scrubbing out toilets an hour earlier, Geoff thought, you'd never have believed it was the same man.

'Thank you again for looking after Dunstan,' he said, standing in the hall with Mrs Baxter and the three boys. 'I hope he hasn't been too much trouble.'

'No trouble at all,' Mrs Baxter assured him. 'They've all been playing on the computer upstairs. Having a lovely time. Did you get your emergency delivery off to Preston?'

'We did indeed, thank you,' said Alan. He beamed down at Tom and Geoff. 'And I'm sorry to have taken up your Saturday morning. Perhaps I can make it up to you both? How about I take us all bowling tomorrow afternoon?'

'That's very kind,' said Geoff smoothly, 'but I can't go anywhere tomorrow. I have to visit my gran.'

'Never mind,' said Alan. 'What about you, Tom?'

Tom was still trying to think of a reason why he couldn't go when his mother answered for him.

'We'd love to,' she said. 'Tom used to enjoy bowling, but he hasn't been for ages. When shall we meet up?'

Later, when they were back at the Eyrie, Tom asked Geoff why he had said he was visiting his grandmother.

'Your gran lives in Portugal, doesn't she?' he added.

'She does,' Geoff agreed, 'but I didn't really want to go bowling. Thought I'd rather go flying. If that's all right?'

Tom sighed. 'So while I have to go out with Alan, you're going to go swimming in France again or something, are you?'

Geoff grinned. 'Do you mind?'

And Tom didn't really mind. His friend had, after all, spent a lot of time during the week waiting outside Alan's house when they both knew he would much rather have been flying around. And earlier that afternoon he had flown Tom out to the industrial estate and shown him where Alan worked. So it seemed only fair that, while Tom was with Alan on Sunday, Geoff should be free for once to go wherever he wanted.

Tom's only regret was that he wasn't going with him, and he knew exactly whose fault that was. It was

Alan's. It was all Alan's fault. Everything in life had been fine until he had appeared and begun turning everything upside down. *Don't I have a say in any of this?* Tom wanted to ask. *Doesn't anyone want to know what I think?*

But apparently they didn't.

At the bowling on Sunday afternoon, Tom and Dunstan were teamed up against Alan and Tom's mother and, at the start, Dunstan didn't do very well. He was using a ball that was too heavy for him and had just sent it into the gutter for the third time when the mother of the family playing in the next lane leaned across to Tom.

'I hope your dad won't mind my suggesting it,' she said, 'but perhaps your brother would do better with this one.' And she passed across a lighter ball.

It took a moment for Tom to realize that the woman thought they were a family, and he was surprised at how strongly he disliked the idea of anyone thinking that, even for a moment.

'We are not a family,' he told her firmly. 'These are just . . . people I know. We've *never* been a family.'

CHAPTER SIX

Geoff's extra reading lesson at the end of school on Monday was cancelled because Miss Stevenson was away on a course. Tom, however, still had extra science with Mr Bampford.

Geoff offered to wait, but Tom told him not to bother. He knew his friend would much rather be hurtling around the countryside somewhere in Aquila.

'I'll walk home,' he said. 'I've got all those new rocks to sort out, remember? I'll be OK.'

The day before, while Tom had been bowling, Geoff had picked up some odd-looking rocks, on a flight somewhere in the north, that he thought might cheer up his friend after an afternoon with Alan. Tom was almost certain that one of the rocks was a chunk of molybdenite ore – extremely rare in Europe – and he was rather looking forward to checking this in one of his reference books.

'You're sure you don't want me to hang around?'

Geoff asked. 'You don't need Aquila to do your maths or anything?'

'All done yesterday,' said Tom. 'I'll be fine. You have a good flight.'

So Geoff went off in Aquila, and Tom walked over to the physics lab for his lesson with Mr Bampford.

In the lab, however, there was no sign of the science teacher. Instead, he found Miss Taylor sitting at the teacher's desk, waiting for him.

'Slight change of plan,' she said, motioning Tom to a chair in front of her. 'I've told Mr Bampford to go home, because I think you and I need to have a talk. About these.' She held up some sheets of paper, and Tom recognized the top one as the maths homework he had handed in that morning.

'Oh?' There was a slight twitch in Tom's left eye as he spoke.

'Mr Duncan showed them to me this morning. He said you'd got a hundred per cent on all your last three exercises, and he could hardly believe how quickly you picked things up.' Miss Taylor looked carefully at Tom. 'I found it quite hard to believe myself.'

The twitch in Tom's eye became stronger.

'In fact I thought there was a strong possibility that you hadn't picked up anything, and that, instead, you'd got someone to do the maths for you and copied out their answers. Would that be what really happened?'

Tom hesitated, but even hardened criminals in Year 10 knew that there was never any point lying to Miss Taylor. He nodded.

'I thought so.'

Miss Taylor's voice was calm, but Tom gulped nervously as he wondered what she would do next. The Deputy Head had a legendary reputation for fierceness. There was a rumour that, if she shouted at you, the sound of her voice alone was enough to make clumps of your hair fall out.

But Miss Taylor did not shout. Instead, she gave a little sniff and said, simply, 'I suppose it's not entirely your fault.'

'Isn't it?' Tom looked up hopefully.

'I'm guessing,' said Miss Taylor, 'and correct me if I'm wrong, that your life at the moment is very full – full of the things you want to do and the things you want to find out about – and that there's not a lot of time left at the end of the day for extra maths homework. I'm guessing that's why you decided to get some help. Is that right?'

Tom agreed that, yes, it was, pretty much.

'I think Mr Duncan may have been pushing you too hard,' said Miss Taylor regretfully. 'It's a mistake young teachers often make, I'm afraid. They get so excited when they find a student who actually *wants* to learn that they go a bit overboard and . . . anyway, I've had a word with him and Mr Duncan promises in future not to set work beyond your ability.'

There was something in the way she said this that almost made Tom feel rather sorry for the maths teacher.

'But let's get one thing clear . . .' Miss Taylor leaned

forward and looked directly at Tom. 'If ever you are unable to complete an assignment, for whatever reason, you will tell the person concerned, truthfully and honestly, why you couldn't do it and work out a new timetable. You understand? Because if I see any more of this –' she waved at Tom's maths homework as she spoke – 'I will have you hauled up on stage in school assembly and publicly flogged. Do I make myself clear?'

His eye twitching violently, Tom agreed that she had made herself very clear. He knew the Deputy Head probably wasn't serious about the public flogging, but that was the thing about Miss Taylor.

You were never entirely sure.

Halfway home, Tom decided to go up to the water tower. He was still shaking from his encounter with the Deputy Head and, if Geoff was back, it would help to talk to him about what had happened.

The path through the woods that led up the tower was quite often used by dog walkers so Tom checked carefully that he was alone before blowing the three short blasts and two long on his dog whistle that would bring Aquila down from the tower – if it was there.

What happened next was a bit of a shock. He heard a voice with a strong American accent coming from somewhere to his right.

'Whoa!' said the voice. 'How did you do that?'

'Geoff?' said Tom. 'Is that you?'

'Tom!' The voice that answered was definitely Geoff. 'I thought you said you were going home.'

Tom put his hand out. Aquila was there, he could feel it.

'Geoff? Have you got someone in there?'

'He surely has!' It was the other voice again. 'He's got me!'

'Hang on . . .' That was Geoff's voice again and suddenly Aquila blinked into view. Geoff was inside, looking distinctly embarrassed, his finger on the button that had just turned off the invisibility, and beside him in the other seat was a girl.

She was about the same age as the boys, very pretty, and dressed almost entirely in white. She had a white skirt, a white top with pale blue flowers embroidered round the neck, a white band in her hair, white shoes and a white bag attached to one wrist. She smiled cheerfully at Tom.

'Hi there!' She gave a little wave.

'I . . . we . . . I wasn't expecting you,' said Geoff.

Tom was too astonished to speak.

'I'm Paige!' The girl gave another wave. 'Paige Legrand. You must be Tom. I have heard *so* much about you!'

Tom opened his mouth . . . then closed it again.

'You're probably wondering where I've come from,' said Paige. 'Well, Geoff picked me up in Norway, just half an hour ago. I mean! How cool is that!'

'Norway?' Tom finally managed to speak.

'My mom's in the oil business,' said the girl happily, 'but I'm not Norwegian. I'm American. Though you probably guessed that from the accent!'

'Look . . .' Geoff gazed nervously around the woods. 'We can't hang around down here. Why don't you get in and we'll talk about it in the tower.'

Tom hesitated a moment, then climbed into Aquila.

'Hey!' Paige gave a little giggle. 'This is cosy, huh?'

Tom did not answer. As they flew up to the tower, his mind was racing. Geoff had told someone else about Aquila. Rule Number One was that they would never, ever, tell anyone else, and Geoff had broken it. He had told someone.

He had told a girl.

At the top of the tower, almost before Aquila had stopped, Tom climbed out and Geoff followed him to the far side of the room.

'Well?' demanded Tom. 'Were you planning to tell me about this? Eventually?'

'Um, no . . . not really . . .' Geoff blushed. 'I thought you'd rather not know.'

'Rule Number One, Geoff! We both agreed! Never to tell anyone about Aquila. That was Rule Number One!'

'I know,' said Geoff, 'but it's all right, really it is! She won't tell anyone. She promised.'

'Oh, she's *promised*, has she?' said Tom bitterly. 'Well, that's all right then, isn't it? I mean, as long as she's promised not to tell anyone, there's no need to worry, is there?'

'I know how it looks but if you –'

'Oh, noooooo!'

Both boys turned. Paige had climbed out of Aquila

and was studying a smudge of dirt on the hem of her skirt.

'Look at this!' She stared accusingly at the boys. 'How long is it since you guys cleaned in there?'

'That does it,' muttered Tom. 'You can sort this out on your own . . .'

He strode back to Aquila, stepped in and pushed the button that would take him forward out of the window. A second later, he had landed on the ground at the base of the tower, climbed out and started walking away.

Behind him, he could hear Geoff calling to him to come back, and Paige's voice asking, 'Is he upset about something?' but he ignored them both. A part of his brain wondered if he should at least send Aquila back up to the tower so that they could get down, but decided in the same instant not to bother.

If Geoff wanted Aquila, he could whistle for it.

Walking home, as fast as he could, Tom found several thoughts suddenly fitting together in his head like pieces from a jigsaw. Almost the only place that molybdenite was found anywhere in Europe was Norway, and if Geoff had picked up a piece of it there yesterday, that probably meant he had met Paige then.

And then he remembered Miss Taylor had said Geoff had been asking about Norway the week before and that meant . . . that meant Geoff had probably met Paige days ago. Then met her several times since but said nothing about it. Tom wasn't sure which was worse. That his friend had broken Rule Number One and told someone else about Aquila, or that he had done it and kept it a secret. Geoff was supposed to be his friend. They told each other everything . . . At least they used to . . .

Arriving home, Tom saw Alan's silver Lexus parked in the driveway. That was all he needed, he thought, a cheery conversation with his mother and Alan, asking how his day had been. He let himself in the back door and got himself a glass of water from the tap in the kitchen and it was while he was standing there that he saw, out of the window, his mother and Alan in the garden.

They were kissing.

Some days, thought Tom, you couldn't help wishing you'd never got out of bed.

When Mrs Baxter answered the knock at the back door, she found Geoff standing outside. She was a little surprised – he didn't usually call round this late on a school night – but on this occasion at least she was very glad to see him.

'You're just the person I need,' she said, pulling him inside. 'Tom's very upset.'

'Is he?' asked Geoff.

'Yes.' Mrs Baxter's face had a worried look as she closed the door. 'But we don't know why. When he got home from school, we could see something was wrong but he wouldn't say what it was.'

'Ah . . .' said Geoff.

'He just went straight up to his room and said he didn't want to talk to anyone.' She lowered her voice. 'He's cataloguing his rocks again, and he hasn't done that for ages. You can hear him muttering to himself up there, marching up and down his room. He sounds really *angry* about something.'

'Does he . . .?' said Geoff.

'Do you think you could try to talk to him?' asked Mrs Baxter. 'Get him to tell you what the trouble is?'

Geoff agreed that he would try.

'I'm sure, whatever it is, he'll tell you about it,' said Mrs Baxter. 'You two don't have any secrets from each other, do you? You never have.'

CHAPTER SEVEN

Up in his bedroom, Tom tried to sort his collection of rocks by their weight in the table of elements rather than simple geological age. Sorting his rocks was something that usually helped when he was upset, but at the moment it didn't seem to be working. He'd pick up a piece of marcasite and, instead of looking up its mineral content, he'd see a picture in his head of Miss Taylor waving his homework, or Paige sitting in Aquila, or his mother in the garden with Alan . . .

He glanced up briefly when Geoff came in, but then went back to studying the piece of marcasite.

'I'm sorry,' said Geoff. 'I know I should have told you, but . . . well, I'm sorry.'

Tom did not answer.

'Maybe, if I explain what happened,' said Geoff, 'and how I met her and . . .'

'I don't want to know!' Tom interrupted. 'I don't

want to know anything about her. In fact I'd prefer it if you never mentioned her ever again.'

'No,' said Geoff. 'Right.'

There was a long pause.

'So how *did* you meet her?' asked Tom.

'It was in France,' said Geoff.

'France?' Tom stared at him.

'You remember the Sunday I went swimming and got the sunburn? It was then. She was on holiday there and saw me getting out of Aquila.' Geoff sighed. 'I thought I'd checked everywhere. I thought there was no one around. But when I was walking down to the water, there she suddenly was, asking how I could step out of thin air like that.'

'And you told her?'

'I thought if I explained things, she might understand how important it was not to tell anyone else.' Geoff took a deep breath and sat down on the end of Tom's bed. 'So we chatted for a bit, went for a swim, she bought me lunch . . . and then when I had to go, she gave me her address in Norway and said if I was ever flying that way, I should call in.'

'So you did,' said Tom.

'You were out bowling.' Geoff looked rather sheepish. 'I didn't think it'd do any harm.'

He had in fact been rather proud of the navigation that took him to Paige's house in Stavanger. It was quite an achievement for someone who had problems reading signs in English, let alone Norwegian, and when he had found Paige she had been so excited to see him, so impressed that he had flown on his own across the North Sea, so amazed at the sight of Aquila – and had pleaded for a chance to fly in it herself.

Geoff had agreed to take her up for a quick flight around the town and Paige had loved every second of it. She had shrieked with pleasure as they buzzed the tops of the houses on their way across town. She had laughed out loud as they swooped down to the sea and along the coast a few miles to the north, and she had gone quiet in stunned amazement as Geoff paused Aquila a few metres above the waves as the huge dorsal fin of an orca whale made its way through the water.

One way and another it had been a very pleasant afternoon and Paige had begged him to come back another time. Geoff agreed, and then she had begged to be allowed to see the Eyrie . . .

'Is that where you left her?' asked Tom. 'At the Eyrie?'

'No, no, I took her home.' Geoff stood up and walked to the window. 'And I've told her it'd be best if I didn't see her again. After Saturday.'

Tom looked at him. 'Saturday?'

'I'd already promised to take her to London on Saturday before you turned up,' Geoff explained. 'She wants to go shopping.'

'Shopping,' muttered Tom. 'Of course.'

'It's while your mum's having her party,' said Geoff. 'I didn't think you'd mind.'

Tom said nothing.

'I'm sorry,' said Geoff eventually. 'I don't know what else to say. I'm sorry.'

The days that followed were not easy. Geoff had said he was sorry, and Tom had said it was all right, but things between them were not the same. The fact was Tom thought Geoff should not have told Paige about Aquila and, deep down, Geoff knew that Tom was right.

When they were together, however, they tried to behave as if nothing had changed. They flew to school together in the mornings, and then back at the end of the day – but things *had* changed, and perhaps it was as well that, for most of the week, Tom had to go straight home after school to help his mother prepare for her party.

Throughout the week, Mrs Baxter was busy with a long list of things that needed to be done, including shopping, cooking food, cleaning the house, tidying the garden and borrowing huge quantities of china and glass from Mrs Murphy next door – and Tom was required to help.

His main job was looking after Dunstan, because the person who was really helping Mrs Baxter was Alan. Every evening, the silver Lexus would glide into the driveway and Alan would step out and immediately set about building a barbecue, or setting up a large tent at the bottom of the garden in case it rained, or going to the shops and coming back with crates of drink and bread rolls that Mrs Baxter stacked in the dining room and round the kitchen – leaving Tom to look after his son.

It was not a demanding job – all you had to do with Dunstan was sit him in front of a computer and occasionally feed him a different game – but it was not what Tom wanted to be doing. Being with someone who was four years younger and hardly ever spoke was not like being with Geoff at the Eyrie. Nothing was.

Tom's mother kept saying how kind it was of Alan to come and help and how she would never have managed without him, but that was not how Tom saw the situation. As the days passed, Alan seemed to be moving more and more into their lives and Tom was increasingly convinced that he was planning, one day, to move in for good.

On Saturday, after a morning spent laying out tables and chairs, napkins and glasses, bottles and food, the guests started arriving at about midday. There were a lot of them – elderly relations like Tom's Great-aunt Sarah from Northumberland, neighbours from all along the street like Mrs Murphy, friends that Mrs Baxter had known at school and college . . .

And of course there was Alan.

Except that Alan wasn't really one of the guests. As he watched his mother welcoming people and offering them drinks, Tom noticed that Alan was doing the same. And when it came to dishing out food and passing round plates, Alan was doing that as well.

As the party progressed, Tom saw how his mother

would talk to someone and then take them to meet Alan. A few minutes later, she'd get someone else and bring them over . . . to meet Alan. This wasn't a party to celebrate his mum recovering from agoraphobia, Tom realized. Its real purpose was for all her friends to have a chance to meet Alan.

'What do you think of him then?'

Old Mrs Murphy had appeared beside Tom and was nodding in Alan's direction.

'Your mother's young man. I think he's rather nice.'

Tom did not answer.

'And she deserves someone after all this time, she really does.' Mrs Murphy peered short-sightedly across the grass to where Alan was at work on the barbecue. 'What does he do for a living, do you know?'

'No,' said Tom. 'I don't know anything about him.' And he turned and went indoors.

Up in his bedroom, Tom found Dunstan sitting at the computer. He didn't look up or speak as Tom came in, simply carried on with his game, and Tom lay on his bed, staring up at the ceiling.

At this moment, he thought gloomily, Geoff and Paige would be in London. In his mind's eye he could see them sitting in Aquila, swooping around the sights of the capital city, laughing, enjoying themselves . . .

As it happened, Geoff was not in London at that time, and nor was he enjoying himself as much as he'd hoped. His day had not gone the way he had planned.

The plan had been to fly to Norway, pick up Paige,

take her to London and spend the afternoon showing her the sights and letting her do some shopping. Unfortunately, that was not what had happened.

To start with, Miss Stevenson had rung Geoff's parents the evening before to say that she would be back from her course by lunchtime on Saturday and could give Geoff his extra reading lesson at two o'clock that afternoon. It meant the time Geoff could spend in London with Paige was severely shortened. By the time he had flown her to and from Norway, they would have barely an hour and a half.

Then, when Geoff arrived at Paige's house in Stavanger at the arranged time, there was no sign of Paige. He waited twenty minutes, and was debating whether he should go up to the house and knock on the door, when she came tripping down the garden in a dressing gown and slippers. He climbed out of Aquila to meet her and Paige explained that she had got to bed very late last night and had only just woken up.

'But I am *so* looking forward to this!' she said. 'I just need to get dressed. Give me two minutes!'

She returned thirty minutes later – how anyone could take thirty minutes to get dressed was a mystery to Geoff – and did a little twirl on the grass.

'What do you think?' she said. 'Is it all right?'

'Is what all right?' asked Geoff.

'The outfit!' Paige was dressed in pink that day, with matching shoes and hair-band, and a large expensive-looking bag slung over her shoulder. 'Does it look OK?'

'Yes, it's fine,' said Geoff. 'Can we go now?'

Crossing the English coast somewhere over Norfolk on their way to London, Paige asked if there was anything to eat or drink.

'Only I missed breakfast, you see,' she explained. 'In all the rush.'

Geoff produced a can of drink and a packet of crisps from his backpack, but when he opened the can, the contents fizzed out and splashed over Paige's trousers.

Geoff tried to tell her that it didn't matter, but apparently it mattered to Paige, who said determinedly that she was not going anywhere until she had had a chance to clean up.

Geoff changed course and flew to the Eyrie, where he found a bucket of water and a towel, but Paige was still not happy.

'You mean you don't have *any* cleaning products here?' She looked around the Eyrie in disbelief. 'Are you serious?'

Geoff said they seemed to manage without, most of the time.

'OK,' said Paige. 'I guess I'll just have to get changed.'

'We don't have much for you to get changed into,' said Geoff. 'I think Tom may have left a sweater here, but . . .' He stopped, noticing that Paige had reached into her bag and taken out a pile of clothes. 'Right . . .' he said. 'I'll go and stand over here.'

He retreated to the back of the Eyrie, wondering what sort of person went out for the day with a bag containing a change of clothing, and it was while he was there, carefully studying Tom's collection of mountain peaks, that Paige called out to him.

'It's trying to say something.'

'What?' Glancing over his shoulder, Geoff could see there were words flashing in the air above the dash in Aquila. 'What does it say?'

'It's asking if it can . . .' Paige paused a moment before reading the words: '. . . *revanigrate the hydro-morphic energizers.* What does that mean?'

'Ask it if it thinks it's a good idea,' said Geoff. He was a little reluctant to come back to Aquila until Paige had finished getting changed.

'It says yes.'

'OK.' Geoff nodded. 'Tell it to go ahead.'

Aquila often asked permission to change a setting or adjust a control and, as long as the lifepod said it was a good idea, they usually let it do what it wanted.

When Paige told him it was all right and he could come back, Geoff found she was now wearing a yellow dress, and that she had changed both the band in her hair and her shoes, so that they matched the new outfit.

'Right.' He climbed back into Aquila. 'Let's try again.' He reached out for the controls and that was when he noticed that most of the lights on the dash had gone out.

'What happened?' he asked. 'What did you do?'

'I didn't do anything!' said Paige. 'I was just sitting here getting changed!'

Geoff pressed the small green light, third in from

70

the left, and the words 'HI! WHAT CAN I DO FOR YOU?' appeared rather faintly in front of him.

'What's happened?' he asked.

More words flashed up. A lot of words.

'Oops,' said Paige as she studied them. 'That's not good, is it?'

Lying on his bed, listening to the noise of the party coming up from the garden, Tom became aware of another sound – of someone hurrying up the stairs, then along the landing towards his room. Whoever it was, he thought, and whatever they wanted, he would tell them to go away and the words were forming in his mouth as the door burst open.

'You've got to come quickly!' Geoff's face was pale and anxious. 'Something's happened to Aquila!'

'What?' Tom swung his legs off the bed. 'What's happened?'

Geoff was about to tell him when he noticed Dunstan. 'I'll tell you outside,' he said. 'Come on!'

On the way downstairs, Geoff gave Tom a brief account of what had happened at the Eyrie.

'I knew this'd happen,' Tom muttered as he followed Geoff out of the front door and round the side of the house to where Aquila was parked in front of the garage. 'She's broken it, hasn't she?'

'I keep telling you, I didn't do anything!' Paige stood up so that the top part of her body appeared in the air above an invisible Aquila. 'I was just sitting there getting changed.'

71

'She's right,' said Geoff. 'It wasn't her fault. Really. But something's happened. It won't go faster than a walk now, however hard you push the button. It took us ten minutes to get here . . .'

Tom swung himself into Aquila, pressed the small green button and asked what had happened. The explanation that scrolled up on the screen in front of him was a long one and contained sections about how '*the hyper field output has been temporarily bypassed until the toroid balance has been restored to its optimal setting* . . .', which Tom did not understand at all. The overall meaning, however, was clear enough.

'Well?' asked Geoff urgently when he had finished.

'Well,' said Tom, 'as far as I can tell, Aquila is giving itself a sort of service, and it had to turn off a lot of its functions while it's doing it. But it's not *too* bad. Everything should be back to normal in a couple of hours.'

'A couple of hours!' said Geoff. 'Are you serious? How am I going to get Paige back to Norway?'

'You can fly her there,' said Tom. 'Just not for two hours, that's all.'

'If I'm not back by three thirty,' said Paige, 'my mom'll start screaming.'

Tom looked at his watch. 'That should be all right. How long does it take to get to Norway? Twenty minutes?'

'It's too late,' said Geoff. 'I have my lesson with Miss Stevenson at two, and if I don't turn up for it Miss Taylor'll want to know why. And we can't have her asking questions. Not again.'

72

Both Paige and Geoff were looking expectantly at Tom, and it was a moment before he realized why.

'No,' he said firmly. 'No. Absolutely not. I'm not taking you anywhere.' He turned to Geoff. 'She's your problem, not mine . . .'

CHAPTER EIGHT

'You *have* to take her,' said Geoff. 'There's no other choice . . .'

'I guess there is *one* other choice,' Paige suggested. 'I could fly Aquila myself, couldn't I? I mean, all I have to do is tell it where to go, right? Then, when I get home, I can tell it to fly itself back to you. It can do that, can't it?'

The image flashed into Tom's head of Paige flying off in Aquila and that being the last they ever saw of it.

'No,' he found himself saying. 'No. I'll take you.'

Geoff gave a sigh of relief. 'OK! Great! Well, I'll take Paige back to the Eyrie and then you can . . .'

'Is that a barbecue?' Paige's delicate nose was sniffing the air. 'Do I smell food?'

'Mum's giving a party,' Tom explained, 'but you can't . . .'

'I am *so* starving!' Paige was already out of Aquila

and walking round the side of the house to the back garden. 'Geoff was in such a hurry this morning, I didn't have any breakfast.' A moment later she was in the garden staring around at the guests. 'Which one's your mom?'

'She's over there.' Tom pointed. 'But like I said, you can't . . .'

But apparently Paige could. She was already making her way through the guests towards Mrs Baxter, and all Tom and Geoff could do was follow her.

Tom's mother was delighted to see them. She knew Tom had not been enjoying himself and was relieved to see that Geoff had persuaded him down from his room.

'I thought you couldn't come today,' she said. 'Tom said you were out with a friend.'

'That'll be me.' Paige extended a hand. 'Paige Legrand. I hope you don't mind my tagging along!'

'Any friend of Geoff's is welcome here!' Mrs Baxter beamed. 'Have you known each other long?'

'We met on holiday,' said Paige easily. 'And now I'm touring England for a bit. Are you sure it's all right for me to gatecrash like this?'

'Of course it is!' said Mrs Baxter, warmly. 'Come and get some food. And you can tell me where you got that lovely dress . . .'

Paige was good at parties. Watching her move around, chatting to different people, laughing and looking completely relaxed, you'd have thought she was with people she'd known all her life. Everybody seemed to like her and even Mrs Murphy came over and told Tom how lucky he was to have such a nice girl for a friend.

An hour later, when it was time for Geoff to go to his lesson with Miss Stevenson, it was Paige who solved the problem of explaining why Tom needed to go with them.

'Would it be OK,' she asked Mrs Baxter, 'if Tom took me back to where I'm staying?'

Tom was half expecting his mother to say no, and that he was needed to keep an eye on Dunstan. But she didn't.

'Yes, of course,' she agreed. 'That'll be fine.'

'That is *so* great!' Paige produced a dazzling smile. 'And will it be OK if he stays for an hour or so? To meet my parents, and say hi and that?'

Mrs Baxter assured her that would be fine too, and Tom found himself wondering if anyone ever said no to Paige.

They flew to Miss Stevenson's house first, to drop Geoff off for his lesson, and then Tom took Paige back to the Eyrie.

At the water tower, there was still half an hour before Aquila came back online and they could fly to Norway and, given that Tom had made it clear he didn't much like Paige, this could have been a rather awkward time.

Paige, however, seemed completely unembarrassed. She walked around the Eyrie, examining the contents of the shelves and chattering away exactly as she had done at the party. She loved the Eyrie, she said. She loved the way they had decorated it and she wanted to know all about Tom's collection of mountain peaks. Almost despite himself, Tom found himself drawn into conversation. He told her how they had used Aquila's laser to slice off the sections of rock, and then found himself telling her about school, and Miss Taylor, and even about his mother.

'And what about your dad?' Paige asked. 'What does he do?'

'He left,' Tom told her, 'when I was three.'

'No kidding!' Paige was sitting on the sofa, her knees tucked up under her chin. 'Same age mine left me! Do you hear from him at all?'

'I get a card and some money,' said Tom. 'At Christmas and on my birthday.'

'Me too.' Paige nodded. 'So did your mom get married again?'

Tom shook his head.

'What about this Alan guy? Looked to me like they were kinda close.'

Tom admitted it was beginning to look that way to him, and then found himself telling Paige about the day he had first found Alan in the sitting room, and hoped he was just a friend but how events had slowly made it clear that he was more than that.

'Been there!' Paige nodded sympathetically. 'Been there and done that more than once.' She chuckled briefly, then looked serious. 'And you know the worst

77

thing? This person walks into your life, into your home, where you've been living quite happily, just the two of you, and you want to say, Hold on a second! Don't I have a say in this? But apparently you don't.'

'Yes!' said Tom. 'Yes, that's it exactly!'

'And the next thing you know your mom's talking about getting married and you don't really know anything about the guy. I mean, he could be a bank robber for all you know – and now he's coming to live with you!'

Tom said he knew exactly what she meant. 'Is that what happened to you?' he added.

'Three times,' said Paige.

Tom was interested, despite himself. 'Did you mind?'

'I did the first time.' Paige sniffed. 'I was only seven. Second one I never actually met – that only lasted six hours – and the one she's got now . . . Dan . . . he's OK. What about this Alan guy, is he all right? What does he do for a living?'

'He cleans toilets,' said Tom.

'Are you sure?' Paige frowned. 'That suit he was wearing was kind of expensive for a janitor.'

'I don't know if that's all he does,' said Tom. 'I don't really know anything about him. I don't talk to him unless I have to.'

'Ah . . .' Paige nodded. 'I tried that with Number One. Big mistake.'

'Was it?'

'Thing is,' said Paige, 'situations like that, you need

all the information you can get. It's no good giving him the silent treatment. It's not going to work. You want to ask him lots of questions – and I mean *lots*. You need to find out what he does, where he works, what he likes . . . You want to know *everything.*'

Tom considered this.

'And the other thing you need to do,' Paige went on, 'is watch what he's like with your mom. I mean, does he make her happy? Does he make her laugh? Because if he does, then you might as well not bother fighting, because you're not going to win. You're better off working out if there's anything in it for you. I got a complete new wardrobe out of Dan.'

Sitting the other end of the sofa, Tom looked at Paige with a new respect. He was beginning to understand why Geoff had flown all the way to Norway to see her.

At twenty-eight minutes past two, all the lights came back on in Aquila. Tom asked if everything was back to normal and the words 'ALL FINE AND DANDY, THANKS!' flashed up in front of him in bright letters. Paige gathered up her things and Tom took the controls.

He rather enjoyed the flight to Norway. Navigating to Stavanger was simple enough as Geoff had given him the course and the co-ordinates he needed, and although they ran through a thunderstorm somewhere off the coast of Lincoln, the skies cleared as they crossed the North Sea, and racing over the water at a few hundred feet with the sun glinting on the waves below was rather exciting.

They talked the whole way. Paige told Tom a long and embarrassing story about how a diary she kept had been discovered by her mother and Tom told Paige how he had kept a diary about finding Aquila that had been discovered by Miss Taylor – who fortunately didn't believe it. Then they swapped more stories about schools and parents, which all seemed to involve a lot of laughing, and when they finally found themselves hovering above Stavanger and Paige was pointing out her house – which was bigger than anything Tom had seen in his life – he was almost disappointed that the trip was over.

'Well . . . thanks for the ride home!' said Paige as Tom brought Aquila to a stop in a section of the enormous garden where she could climb out without being seen. 'It was fun.' She picked up her bag and added, 'Would you like to come to my party next week?'

'Party?' said Tom.

'It's my birthday,' Paige explained. 'Mom's giving me a party here – goes on all afternoon, hundreds of people – but if you and Geoff could come it'd be just great.' She smiled, appealingly. 'You think you could?'

And Tom heard himself saying that he'd have to ask Geoff but, yes, he thought they might be able to manage that.

'You are such a sweetie!' Paige leaned across and gave him hug. 'See you next week then!' She went racing up the garden towards the house, pausing at the top of some steps to give him a wave and one last radiant smile.

After she'd gone, Tom sat in the cockpit of Aquila for some time before eventually pressing the green button and asking it to fly him back to the Eyrie. He wondered, as he did so, what Geoff would say when he told him about the party.

When he got home, there were still some guests from his mother's party sitting around the garden and lying on the grass. His mother was just coming out of the kitchen with a large pot of tea, looking rather cheerful.

'Did Paige get back all right?' she asked.

Tom said that she had.

'She was a nice girl,' said Mrs Baxter. 'Will you see her again?'

'Maybe,' said Tom. 'I'm not sure.'

Alan was over by the barbecue doing some sausages for a hot dog for Dunstan, who had been so busy on the computer he had forgotten to eat.

'You want one, Tom?' he called across, and Tom realized he hadn't eaten a great deal himself and said, yes, thank you, he would.

He joined the others on the grass, chatting in the afternoon sun, and it all felt very relaxed and easy. At one point someone organized a group playing with a frisbee, and later on there was a game of poker which they played with monopoly money and Dunstan won eighteen thousand pounds. Somehow, it was all very *comfortable*, and then Geoff arrived.

He was anxious to hear if Paige had got back to Norway all right. Tom assured him that she had, and then told him about the birthday party.

'A party? Really? What did you say?'

'I told her we might manage it,' said Tom. 'We're not doing anything else on Saturday, are we?'

And suddenly, Tom didn't know why, everything was all right between them again. It was back to how it had been before. The bad feelings had disappeared and Geoff was his friend again, just as he'd always been.

When the party finally broke up late that afternoon, everyone seemed to be happy. Mrs Murphy was the last to leave and she was almost too happy to walk straight. Mrs Baxter was happy that her party had been such a success. Alan was happy for Mrs Baxter, and Dunstan was still happily clutching his eighteen thousand pounds.

Everyone was happy, and the feeling that, somehow, things might be going all right continued through the rest of the weekend and well into the week that followed.

It lasted, in fact, right up to the time that Dunstan went missing.

CHAPTER NINE

Tom and Geoff were sitting in the Eyrie after school on Wednesday when Tom got a phone call from his mother.

'Dunstan's disappeared,' she told him. 'He walked out of the house after lunch and nobody's seen him since. He's not with you, is he?'

'No,' said Tom. 'Why would he be?'

'He left a note,' said Mrs Baxter, 'saying he was coming over to our house to see you.'

Normally, Dunstan would have been at school, but that day the school had been closed because of a burst water main and he had been sent home.

A little before two o'clock, he had apparently decided he wanted to see Tom, and simply walked out of the house. It was ten minutes before Mrs Munns, the woman looking after him, noticed he was missing, and when she found the note and ran out to call him back, it was too late. There was no sign of him.

Mrs Munns had driven a mile along the road to Tom's house and back again without finding him, then phoned Alan at work to tell him what had happened. Alan had phoned Mrs Baxter to ask if Dunstan had turned up yet, then phoned the police and then gone out on the road himself to find his son.

'I'm going out myself now,' said Mrs Baxter. 'The more of us looking, the more likely we are to find him. Where are you?'

'I'm with Geoff,' Tom told her.

'Well, perhaps you'd better stay there,' said his mother, 'but I'm leaving Mrs Murphy here if you want to come home. I've asked her to come over in case Dunstan turns up while I'm out.'

It was Geoff who suggested – after Tom told him what had happened – that if you wanted to search for a missing eight-year-old boy, it was the sort of thing that would be a lot easier to do from the air.

Before they started, the boys had a brief debate on what would be the best way to conduct the search. Geoff thought they should fly round in a spiral from the last place Dunstan had been seen, while Tom thought it would be better to fly along the route he had probably followed. It was a difficult choice, and there was also the problem of whether it would be better to fly high, to get a wide view, or low enough so they could see people's faces. They were still debating both issues when Geoff suddenly leaned forward and pressed the small green light on the dash.

'HI! WHAT CAN I DO FOR YOU?' appeared in the air in front of them.

'We need to find Dunstan,' Geoff explained. 'D'you know who I mean? The boy that was round at Tom's house every evening last week?'

A picture of Dunstan sitting at Tom's computer appeared in the air in front of them, with 'THIS ONE?' written underneath.

'That's him,' said Geoff. 'He was supposed to be going from a house in Walnut Close to where Tom lives, but it looks like he got lost on the way. Can you find him?'

'SEARCH INITIATED.'

At the same time as the words appeared on the screen, the lifepod shot forward out of the water tower and then up into the air. At several hundred feet, it stopped, swung its nose first to the right, then the left, moved forward, then back and then . . .

'TARGET IDENTIFIED.'

. . . Aquila went into a smooth dive that took them down to a road that ran along the back of their school, where it stopped a few metres in the air directly in front of Dunstan, who was sitting on a low wall, studying the screen of his mobile phone. It was yet another impressive display of the lifepod's abilities, thought Tom. If he'd known Aquila could find missing people so easily, he wouldn't have had to panic that time in New York.

Geoff steered Aquila to a point out of sight behind some bushes. He and Tom climbed out and they walked back to Dunstan.

'What are you doing out here, Dunstan?' Geoff asked.

Dunstan looked up from his phone. 'I was coming to see Tom.'

'You've been missing for two hours,' said Tom. 'What happened? Did you get lost or something?'

'Well . . .' Dunstan looked vaguely around.

'Your dad's been going wild,' said Geoff. 'The police, Tom's mum – everyone's out looking for you. They think you've been kidnapped or something.'

Dunstan frowned. 'I left a note.'

'The note said you were coming to my house,' said Tom, 'but you're not there, are you? And you didn't tell anyone you were lost.' He pointed to the mobile Dunstan was holding. 'How about you phone your dad, and tell him you're OK?'

Dunstan dialled a number on his phone and held it to his ear.

'Dad?' he said. 'It's me.'

There was a pause while he listened to his father and then he turned to Tom and Geoff. 'Where am I?'

Tom took the phone.

'Hello, Alan? We're in Twyford Avenue. It runs along the back of the school and . . . Yes, he's fine . . . Yes . . . Right.' He turned off the phone and gave it back to Dunstan. 'He says to wait here. He'll be round in three minutes.'

In fact it was less than two minutes before the big silver Lexus came barrelling down the road towards them, and Alan jumped out. He hurried over to Dunstan.

'Are you all right?' he asked.

Dunstan nodded.

'You're sure?'

Dunstan nodded again.

Alan took a long deep breath and let it out again. 'So . . . what were you doing?'

'I wanted to see Tom,' said Dunstan. 'I left a note.'

'I know you did,' said Alan, 'but you can't just . . .' He stopped and took another deep breath. 'We'll talk about why it wasn't a good idea when we get home. You hop in the car.' As Dunstan walked over to the car, Alan turned to Tom and Geoff. 'How did you find him?'

'We were just lucky, really,' said Geoff.

'We came out to help look,' said Tom, 'and there he was.'

'Well, thank goodness you did.' Alan ran his fingers through his hair. 'I can't believe he just walked out of the house without a word to anyone . . .'

'Are you going to be very cross with him?' asked Tom.

'Getting cross doesn't really work with Dunstan,' said Alan. 'He's . . . different. You have to give him a reason if you want him to behave in a particular way. And you have to be very precise. His teachers say he's a genius, but when he does things like this it's not easy to believe . . .' He reached into his pocket and took out his phone. 'I'd better call the police. And your mother. Then I'll give you a lift home.'

'No, no, it's OK,' said Tom.

'We do this route every day,' said Geoff.

87

'Are you sure?' Alan looked keenly at the boys then suddenly held out a hand. 'I haven't even said thank you. I owe you one for this. Both of you. I won't forget.'

'I wonder if he meant money,' said Geoff, as they walked round the corner. They both still occasionally wondered how they could use Aquila to make money, but had never managed to come up with an answer.

Geoff blew the signal on his whistle that would bring Aquila down to his right. 'That'd be kind of convenient, wouldn't it?'

That evening, Alan brought Dunstan round to Tom's house so that he could say sorry to Mrs Baxter for all the trouble he'd caused and hand over a bunch of flowers by way of apology. Mrs Baxter invited them both in and then made some scrambled eggs when she found they hadn't eaten. It was while they were all sitting in the kitchen that Tom remembered what Paige had said about it being a good idea to find out as much as possible about Alan . . . and asked him what he did for a living.

He wasn't quite sure what Alan would say – whether he'd try to avoid the question in some way or make up an answer that wasn't true – but he did neither of those things.

'Drains,' he replied promptly. 'Drains and toilets, that's my game! If you're having trouble with back-up or you need some outside loos for a garden party, I'm your man! I've got a little place up on the industrial estate.'

'It's not a "little" place.' Mrs Baxter turned to Tom. 'It's enormous.'

'Have you seen it?' Tom asked.

'Alan showed me round a few weeks back,' said Mrs Baxter. 'You should ask him to give you a tour one day. It's really interesting!'

'A tour . . .' said Tom. 'Yes, I'd like that.'

'You would?' Alan looked surprised. 'Really?'

'Yes,' said Tom. 'Yes, definitely.'

'How about Friday then?' Alan suggested. 'I could pick you up after school.'

'And you could get Geoff to go along with you,' said Mrs Baxter. 'I'm sure he'd be interested as well.'

To their surprise, both boys enjoyed their tour of Alan's business. He picked them up after school on Friday as he had promised, drove them out to the industrial estate and showed them around Unit 17.

He showed them drainage pipes and explained how they got blocked and what you did to unblock them. He showed them septic tanks and explained how they were emptied, and how all the waste could now be recycled. And, finally, he showed them the rows of portaloos behind the main building.

'Probably our biggest money spinner at the moment,' he explained, patting the side of one of the green booths. 'We've got three hundred of them now and, this time of year, they'll all be in use.'

'Who cleans them?' asked Tom.

'I've got a team of people to do that.' Alan said. 'But

if it's a fast turn-around, everybody drops what they're doing and gets stuck in.'

'Everybody?' said Tom. 'Even you?'

'Especially me!' Alan grinned. 'Everyone enjoys seeing the boss get his hands dirty!'

The tour over, he took them up to his office, where his secretary had laid out a plate of buns and some soft drinks for the boys and a large mug of tea for Alan.

Then Geoff asked if he had always been interested in drains and Alan laughed and said no.

'It was Miss Taylor got me into the business,' he added.

'Miss Taylor?' Tom blinked. 'Our Miss Taylor? From school?'

'That's right.' Alan spooned sugar into his tea and stirred it. 'She was my class teacher back then, and at the end of my last term she gave me a card and said, "This is a man I know who clears drains. Go and see him, and if he offers you a job, take it." So I did.'

'Miss Taylor told you to get a job cleaning drains,' said Geoff, 'and you just did what she said?'

'She was quite a forceful woman in those days,' said Alan. 'Most people did what she told them to.'

'And you didn't you mind?' asked Geoff. 'Her telling you what to do?'

'Mind?' Alan chuckled. 'I've never been so grateful to anyone in my life. She laid it all out for me. "Work two years for John," she said, "then set up in business on your own. You'll be good at running a business."' Alan paused, his mug halfway to his lips. 'Nobody'd ever said anything like that to me before. Nobody'd ever told me I'd be good at anything.' He sipped his tea for a moment and added, 'Whenever I have a problem, she's still the first person I go to.' He looked over the top of his mug at the boys. 'Have you come across her much yet, at school?'

'A bit,' said Geoff. 'She's . . . um . . .'

'She's quite scary,' said Tom.

'You can say that again.' Alan grinned. 'Twenty years on and she still frightens the daylights out of me!'

As he was driving them home, Alan mentioned again that he would like to do something for the boys as a thank you for finding Dunstan.

'How about I take you both somewhere?' he suggested. 'Maybe this weekend? A theme park perhaps? Or a visit to London?'

'That's very kind of you,' said Tom, 'but not this weekend.'

'We're busy this weekend,' said Geoff. 'We're going to a party.'

CHAPTER TEN

The boys had spent some time debating what presents they should get for Paige's birthday on Saturday. It wasn't easy. As Geoff said, the only thing they knew she was interested in was clothes, but buying her something to wear from what was left of three pounds pocket money a week meant the options were rather limited.

In the end, Geoff made a print of a photo he had taken of himself and Tom in the Eyrie, with just the nose of Aquila visible in the background, and put it in a frame. Tom, meanwhile, used Aquila's laser to slice off a section from the peak of Mont Blanc, glued it to a piece of wood and taped a printed piece of paper on the base explaining what it was.

'At least we know no one else'll be giving her the same thing,' Geoff said as they sat in the Eyrie wrapping both presents in birthday paper Tom had brought from home. 'When does she want us to be there?'

'One o'clock,' Tom told him. 'That's when the party starts. We can leave after your lesson with Miss Stevenson.'

In the event, however, they nearly didn't get to the party at all, because on Saturday morning Alan arrived at Tom's house in a flatbed lorry with eighteen portable toilets strapped to the back.

'I'm really sorry,' he told Mrs Baxter when she came out to meet him, 'but I'm not going to be able to make it this afternoon.'

Mrs Baxter was going to a Bushido demonstration of Japanese swordsmanship at the town hall that afternoon, and had invited Alan to go with her.

'Oh, dear,' she said. 'Has something happened?'

'I've got two drivers off sick.' Alan gestured to the toilets. 'There's no one else to get this lot down to Bedford by two o'clock. I feel really bad about letting you down.'

'Oh, don't worry about that,' said Mrs Baxter reassuringly. 'I'll be fine on my own.' She glanced up at the cab, where a rather unhappy-looking Dunstan was sitting in the passenger seat staring out of the windscreen. 'Are you taking Dunstan with you?'

'Have to, I'm afraid,' said Alan. 'Nowhere else for him to go.'

'But of course there is!' said Mrs Baxter. 'He can stay with us. I'm sure he doesn't want to sit in a lorry all day!'

'But if you're going out . . .'

'That's not till two o'clock,' said Mrs Baxter, 'and

93

I'll get Mrs Murphy to keep an eye on things after that.' She called up to the cab. 'Dunstan? Would you like to . . .?'

But Dunstan was already climbing down from the lorry and marching up the path towards the house.

'Well, that's settled then!' Mrs Baxter smiled. 'Not much doubt about what he wants to do.'

'I seem to be saying rather a lot of thank yous at the moment,' said Alan. 'One day soon I'm going to have to do something special to make up for it.' He smiled. 'You're sure Tom won't mind?'

'Of course he won't,' said Mrs Baxter. 'He'll be glad of the company.'

Tom was horrified. 'I can't look after Dunstan today,' he protested. 'I'm going over to Geoff's!'

'It's all right,' said Mrs Baxter calmly. 'I've rung his parents and asked if Geoff can come round here for a change. They said that was fine.'

'But . . . but . . .'

'There's nothing to get upset about,' said Mrs Baxter. 'You can still do whatever you were going to do. You just do it here instead of at Geoff's house, that's all.'

When Geoff arrived fifteen minutes later, leaving Aquila parked in the garden, Tom told him the news.

'*You* don't have to stay,' he finished gloomily. 'There's no need for both of us to miss the party. You go on your own.'

It was a generous offer, but Geoff said he thought there was still a chance they could both go.

'If we wait till your mum goes out,' he suggested, 'we can fly to Norway then, can't we? Mrs Murphy'll never notice we've gone. She never comes upstairs, does she? And she'll be asleep most of the time anyway.'

'What about Dunstan?' asked Tom.

'We'll ask him if he minds being left behind,' said Geoff. 'I'm sure he won't. He's got the computer, and at least he's not stuck on a lorry.'

Tom considered this. 'How about we don't *ask* him,' he said eventually. 'Let's just *tell* him that's what we're going to do.'

After lunch, when Mrs Baxter had driven off to her Bushido demonstration, and Mrs Murphy was downstairs dozing in front of the television, Tom and Geoff had a brief conversation with Dunstan.

'Here's the deal, Dunstan,' said Geoff. 'We're going out now and we're leaving you here on your own.'

'Just for a couple of hours,' Tom added. 'OK?'

Dunstan nodded.

'But afterwards,' said Geoff, 'you mustn't tell anyone that's what we did.'

Dunstan thought for a moment. 'Why not?'

'Because we'd get into trouble,' said Geoff.

'You don't have to tell any lies or anything,' Tom assured him. 'You just don't say anything about it, OK? If anyone asks if you've had a good time, you say yes. You don't have to say anything about us not being here.'

Dunstan nodded again.

'But you mustn't run off anywhere,' said Geoff, remembering the incident earlier in the week. 'Remember what your dad said about not going out without asking someone, all right?'

'All right,' said Dunstan.

Ten minutes later, Geoff brought Aquila round to the bathroom window, Tom climbed in and they were on their way.

'We've done it again, haven't we?' said Geoff cheerfully as he took Aquila up to two thousand feet and pointed its nose to the north-east.

'What?'

'We've sorted everything out, haven't we?' said Geoff. 'We hit a problem, but we sorted it. We do it all the time!' He gave the instructions for Aquila to fly them to Stavanger and leaned back in his seat, looking rather pleased with himself. 'We didn't know how to get to New York – we worked it out. I got sunburned in France and we needed a story to explain it – we worked it out. We need to get to Norway this afternoon – we work it out . . . It's what we're good at!'

He was right, Tom thought. In a way, working out what to do to get what they wanted was what they had been doing ever since they found Aquila. They had worked out how to fly it, how to bring it home, where to keep it, how it was fuelled . . . And each time they solved a problem, it made them even more confident that they could deal with whatever came up next.

'It's a good feeling, isn't it?' said Geoff.

And Tom agreed that it was a very good feeling indeed.

The party was an astonishing affair. Tom had thought the party his mother gave had been quite a grand occasion, but Paige's birthday was on a different scale altogether.

From the moment Geoff left Aquila in the air at the bottom of the garden and they began making their way towards the house in search of Paige, the boys were assailed on all sides by noise and excitement. The garden, all three acres of it, thronged with hundreds of people, of all ages.

They had only gone a few steps before a waitress appeared, offering them something to eat from a tray, and a few steps later another one offered them something to drink. As well as the guests, they passed a whole series of entertainers – people on stilts, jugglers, knife throwers – it was like walking through a circus. There was even a man with a dog that could do arithmetic. You gave it a sum – like ten minus three – and the dog went straight over and pointed with its paw to the number seven on the ground.

Paige saw them when they were halfway to the house, gave a great shriek of excitement and came racing through the crowds to meet them.

'You made it!' She hugged each of them in turn. 'I thought you weren't going to come! I am *so* happy!'

She looked happy, and looked even happier when she opened the presents they had brought. She said they were her best presents ever – all her other friends had just given her clothes or money – and she was going to keep them on the table by her bed like . . . for ever.

Even making allowances for the fact that Paige always talked like that, she really did seem to be pleased, and Tom noticed that she kept hold of both the photo and the tip of Mont Blanc all the time they were there.

They could only spend an hour, and it sped by. By the time they had met Paige's mother, had something to eat, met some of Paige's friends, watched the conjuror and the man juggling chainsaws, met some more of Paige's friends and had a tour of the house, Tom discovered it was half past three and they needed to be getting home.

They said goodbye and thank you to Paige's mother, who gave them party bags containing, among other things, several DVDs and an MP3 player, and finally made their way, arm in arm with Paige, towards a part of the garden where, hidden behind a hedge, Geoff could call down Aquila.

'Are you *sure* you can't stay?' Paige demanded for the umpteenth time, and when Tom explained again about Dunstan, and his mother getting back from the Bushido demonstration, she added, 'Well, at least promise me you'll come and visit again one day. I'm not letting you go until you promise!'

'Of course we'll come back,' said Tom.

'As soon as we can,' Geoff agreed.

'Oh, you guys are so brilliant!' said Paige, and she flung her arms extravagantly round their necks.

Geoff blew the signal on his whistle that would bring Aquila down from where it had been hovering above their head and felt for the solid shape of Aquila beside him.

'It's not there,' he said.

'What?' said Tom.

'It's not there.' He blew the whistle again, felt for Aquila and . . . nothing.

'What do you mean it's not there?' asked Paige.

'I mean it's not there!' Geoff moved his arms through the air in the place where Aquila was supposed to be and blew the whistle again . . . and again . . . and again. Then Tom tried it. Then they tried using Tom's whistle in case something had happened to Geoff's . . . but the result was always the same. Aquila did not appear.

'Are you sure this is where you left it?' asked Paige. 'Perhaps we're standing by the wrong hedge.'

Geoff looked around the garden to check, but he knew there was no mistake. Even if he was in slightly the wrong place, it shouldn't have made any difference. Aquila was supposed to fly down to beside you from wherever it was and it could hear the signal from half a mile away. He blew the whistle again, as if doing it for the hundredth time would make any difference.

'Could I ask you not to do that?'

Geoff turned round to see the man with the dog that did sums. He came over and spoke in a low voice. 'That is a dog whistle you're blowing there, right?'

'Um . . . yes.' Geoff nodded.

'I thought so.' The man looked around and lowered his voice even further. 'I'm afraid you're blowing the signal for number five.'

'Number five?'

'That's how the trick works, you see?' The man smiled conspiratorially at Paige. 'I have this whistle in my mouth that signals Ulrika here to go to that number. You've been blowing the signal for number five and unfortunately it is spoiling my act.'

It took a moment for the boys to realize what he was talking about. The man was saying that his dog's ability to do sums was a trick. What he really did was tell the dog the answer by secretly blowing on a whistle that he kept in his mouth, with a different signal for each of the ten numbers.

Tom was the first to realize what this meant.

'Is . . . is two long blasts and two short, one of the signals?' he asked, and there was a sick feeling in his stomach as he said it.

The man nodded. 'That's the signal for number nine, but don't tell anyone, please! We don't want to spoil everything, do we?'

Tom nodded faintly. Two long blasts and two short was also the signal that sent Aquila back to the room at the top of the water tower. They used it at the end of each day so that the lifepod would wait in the Eyrie until they called it down the next morning.

Presumably, that was where Aquila was now. The lifepod had heard the signal and obediently sent itself back to wait in the water tower. It had probably been there for most of the last hour.

'Well,' said Geoff, as the man returned to his stand with the dog. 'Looks like we have another problem.' He did his best to smile. 'How are we going to get out of this one then?'

But Tom knew that, this time, they faced a problem that could not be sorted, however hard they thought about it. Aquila was in England, and they were in Norway. There was no way they could change the facts, and no way they could get home. This time the problem they faced had no solution.

It was hard to believe, but it seemed that the whole wonderful adventure was finally over.

CHAPTER ELEVEN

In his heart of hearts, Tom had always known it would end like this. That it was impossible to keep something like Aquila a secret forever and that, one day, the truth would be discovered. In a way, he was surprised they had managed to hide it as long as they had.

Geoff, sitting beside him on the grass, found it less easy to accept. The idea that he had lost Aquila was something he found almost too awful to contemplate. His face was pale, and he stared sightlessly ahead without speaking.

Paige, at first, couldn't see that they had *lost* Aquila at all.

'You know where it is, don't you?' she said. 'It's in England. No one else knows about it. All you have to do is go back and get it!'

'But we *can't*, can we?' said Tom, quietly.

'Sure you can,' Paige insisted. 'You get tickets for a

ferry or a plane – I'll get you the money – then a train once you get to England. It'll take a couple of days but you can do it. I know you can.'

She sounded so determined that, for a moment, Geoff almost believed that it might be possible.

'We'd need an adult to buy the tickets,' he said.

'So we'll find an adult!' Paige answered.

'What about passports?' said Tom.

'What?'

'We'd need passports to get on a plane or a ferry, wouldn't we?' said Tom patiently.

'In that case . . .' Paige hesitated. 'In that case . . .'

'And when we get home,' Tom continued, 'what do we tell everyone? What do we say when they ask where we've been?'

'You don't say anything at all!' said Paige. 'You say you've got that . . . you know, that thing where you can't remember anything. You say it's all a blank.'

Tom shook his head. 'It wouldn't work.' He thought of all the fuss there had been when Dunstan had gone missing for two hours, and then thought what his mother would do if he went missing for two days. The idea that he could come home after that and say he didn't remember anything was never going to happen.

'He's right,' said Geoff reluctantly. 'The police take it very seriously when people our age go missing. We'd have to tell them the truth. Eventually. There'd be no choice.'

'And when we tell them,' said Tom, 'they'll take

Aquila away. There's no way they'd let us keep it. That's why we had Rule Number One.'

'We might as well get it over with.' Geoff stood up. 'Come on, we'll start with your mother. Where is she?'

As it happened, there was no need to go looking for Mrs Legrand, because she was at that moment striding across the lawns towards them.

'Hey, there you are! I was thinking you hadn't gone yet!' She put a hand on her daughter's shoulder as she smiled down at the boys. 'Bad news, I'm afraid. You have to go home. Now!'

'Mom?' Paige took a deep breath. 'Tom and Geoff have something to tell you.'

'Do they?' Mrs Legrand was still smiling. 'Nothing too serious I hope!'

'It is quite,' said Paige. 'They can't go home.'

'They can't?' Mrs Legrand looked puzzled. 'Why not?'

'It's a long story,' said Tom. 'Could we . . . go indoors?'

'Sure,' Mrs Legrand agreed, 'but what about your friend? Do you want him to join us or . . . or would you rather he didn't?'

Tom hesitated. 'Friend?'

'He's pretty anxious you leave right away,' said Mrs Legrand. 'Says there'll be all kinds of trouble if you don't.'

'What friend?' asked Geoff.

'I didn't catch his name.' Mrs Legrand was leading the way through the guests towards the house. 'But he says his dad's getting home soon and you guys need to be there before he is. He's waiting over there.'

She gestured towards the house and Tom stared in disbelief at the little figure at the top of the steps that led down from the terrace.

It was Dunstan.

'He seems to think it's kind of urgent,' said Mrs Legrand, 'but if you really can't go . . .'

'Dunstan?' Geoff was walking towards him. 'What are you doing here?'

'We have to go.' Dunstan lifted his arm and pointed to his watch. 'If we go right away, we can still get home in time.'

'You . . . you think we can get home?' asked Tom.

Dunstan nodded.

'Are you sure?'

Dunstan nodded again.

For a moment, both boys stared at him, and Geoff was the one who recovered first. He turned to Mrs Legrand and held out his hand. 'Thank you again for having us, Mrs Legrand. That was a really good party.'

'Oh . . .' Mrs Legrand took his hand. 'A pleasure . . .'

'Tom?' Geoff nudged his friend.

'Oh, yes! Thank you very much. We have to go now . . .'

It was not until Paige had led them through the house, out the front door and on to the street that Geoff was able to ask the question that was burning in the minds of all three of them.

'Dunstan . . . How did you get here?'

'I came in Aquila.' Dunstan had taken out a mobile phone and was punching in some numbers as he spoke.

'Aquila? You've got it here?'

Dunstan nodded.

'I thought it was just us three who knew about Aquila.' Paige turned to Geoff and then to Tom. 'Did you tell him?'

Both boys shook their heads.

'So how does he know about it?' asked Paige. 'And how did he know you were here? And how did he know to come and get you?'

Tom and Geoff looked at Dunstan.

'It might be best,' he said, 'if I did the explaining on the way.' He had taken a stick from the hedge by the side of the road and tapped the air beside him. There was the familiar sound of it ringing quietly against the hull of the lifepod. 'We really do have to get home. Now.'

'OK, OK!' Paige held up her hands. 'I'll let you go. But if you don't come back and explain it all to me *very* soon, I will *die*!'

Dunstan's explanation took most of the flight home, partly because there was quite a lot of story to tell, and partly because Dunstan was not very good at telling it. Tom and Geoff kept having to make him go back and fill in the bits he had missed out. By the time they were crossing the English coast, however, they had got the bones of what had happened, though they both still had trouble believing it.

Dunstan had seen Aquila that first Saturday when Geoff had knocked on the window. Or at least had realized something odd was happening when a hand appeared out of thin air and tapped at the glass.

'But you didn't say anything!' said Tom.

'Well, I could tell you didn't want me to know about it,' said Dunstan. 'That's why you sent me out to get a glass of water. And when I came back, I saw Geoff talking to you. Well, I saw his head.'

The sight had, not unnaturally, made Dunstan curious. He had thought about it, wondering what he should do, and on the day of Mrs Baxter's party, when he had found himself alone in Tom's room, he had taken the opportunity to look around for an explanation. That was when he had found the exercise book with '*Licet volare si in tergo aquilae volat*' written on the front.

It was the exercise book in which Tom had written all the details of how they'd found Aquila, how they had brought it home and a journal of all the things they had done in it. It was the book that, as Tom had told Paige, had once been found by Miss Taylor. But while she had presumed it was all made up, Dunstan had believed every word, and decided he would like to see inside Aquila for himself.

He knew from Tom's journal that the boys usually flew the lifepod to school, and then left it thirty feet in the air behind the domestic-science block. He also knew that they called it down at the end of the day by blowing three short blasts and two long on a dog whistle, and that this made the lifepod appear somewhere to your right.

So, on the day he had to stay home from school because of the burst water main, and with only Mrs Munns looking after him, Dunstan left a note on the kitchen table saying that he was going round to Tom's house, walked into town, bought a dog whistle from the pet shop, walked to the comprehensive, blew the signal to bring down Aquila and climbed inside.

Tom stared at him. 'This was the day everyone thought you were lost and your dad called the police, right?'

Dunstan nodded.

'So what did you do in it?' asked Geoff. 'Where did you go?'

'I didn't go anywhere,' said Dunstan. 'I'm not very keen on flying. I just wanted to see if it would connect to my computer.'

Tom's jaw dropped a little further.

'And did it?'

'Oh, yes.' Dunstan nodded calmly. As if connecting a laptop to a six-thousand-year-old piece of alien technology was the sort of thing one did all the time.

'How?' asked Geoff. 'How did you do it?'

Dunstan frowned. '*I* didn't do anything really,' he said. 'I just asked Aquila if it could do it for me. It can speak most of the known languages of the galaxy, you see, and I thought if I told it about the wavelength mobile phones used, maybe it could work out the connection. And it did.'

'So you can . . . talk to it? On your phone?'

Dunstan nodded again. 'I just have to dial up the number and –'

'Aquila has a *phone* number?' Tom could not hide his astonishment.

'Two,' said Dunstan. 'One connects it to the phone, and I use the other to talk to it on my computer. That's what I wanted it for really.' He looked up at the boys sitting either side of him. 'I just wanted to ask it things. About where it came from. How it works. You're not angry, are you?'

Tom stared at him. *He's eight years old*, he kept thinking. *He worked all this out and he's only eight years old. No wonder his teachers think he's a genius.*

'No,' said Geoff slowly. 'No, we're not angry. Now tell us what happened today.'

'Today?' Dunstan looked a little vague.

'Today,' Geoff repeated. 'How did you know where we were? How did you know we were in trouble? How did you know to come and rescue us?'

'Oh, that . . .' Dunstan did his thoughtful look again. 'Well, today, when you said you were going out, I thought you were probably going off in Aquila so I used the computer to ask where you'd gone and Aquila said you'd gone to Norway. Then I asked it to tell me when it got back and about an hour later, it did. It said it was back at the water tower, only you weren't in it. Either of you. You were both still in Norway, which was a bit odd.

'So I asked why it had come back and it said it had

received this signal from the dog whistle and I thought maybe there'd been a mistake. Perhaps you'd blown the wrong signal or something and you were stuck in Norway and I thought I'd better check you were all right. I thought of just sending Aquila back on its own, but then I thought I'd better go with it. In case something had happened.

'So I told Aquila to come round and pick me up, told Mrs Murphy I was going out, and then told Aquila to fly to –'

'Hang on,' said Geoff. 'You told Mrs Murphy where you were going?'

'Yes.' Dunstan's expression did not change. 'You said I had to ask permission before I went anywhere, remember?'

'What did you tell her?' Tom asked. 'Exactly.'

'I asked her if it was all right if I went to Norway.'

'And . . . she said you could go?'

'She told me it was fine,' said Dunstan, 'as long as I was back for tea.'

Alan stood beside Mrs Baxter in the kitchen, looking out of the window down the garden. 'How's he been?' he asked.

'All right, I think.' Tom's mother was setting out plates and knives on the table. 'I'm only just back myself.'

'I've been worrying that maybe I shouldn't have left him.' There was a slightly anxious look on Alan's face. 'Not for that long anyway. Dunstan's not always easy to look after and if he and Tom had an argument . . .'

'They don't seem to be arguing.' Mrs Baxter pointed out of the window to where Tom, Geoff and Dunstan were sitting in the shade of a cherry tree. Tom and Geoff were listening patiently, while Dunstan seemed to be explaining something about his mobile phone.

'I know, but . . .' Alan still sounded doubtful. 'It's quite important they get on together, isn't it? And if they didn't –'

'Well, let's go and find out, shall we?' Mrs Baxter took Alan's hand and led him outside. 'You can ask them if they've enjoyed themselves.'

'So . . . what have you all been doing?' Alan asked, looking down at the boys. 'Have you had a good time?'

Mrs Baxter smiled at Dunstan. 'Mrs Murphy says you asked permission to go to Norway. That's quite a long way, isn't it? What were you doing there?'

Dunstan did not answer immediately.

'Dunstan?' said Alan. 'Mrs Baxter asked you a question.'

'He had to come and rescue us,' said Geoff. 'Tom and I had flown out there, but we couldn't get back because we lost our flying machine. So Dunstan came out and rescued us.'

'Did he now?' Alan smiled down at his son. 'Well, that sounds like quite an adventure!'

'Yes, it was,' Dunstan agreed. 'I'm hungry now. Can I have something to eat?'

'Of course you can!' Mrs Baxter said. 'Tea's laid. Tom, take him inside, will you?'

She watched as the three boys walked up the garden

towards the house. 'I don't think you need to worry too much about them,' she said. 'It looks to me like they're getting on really well together.'

And Alan, as he watched the boys go into the house, still deep in conversation, had to agree that it did.

CHAPTER TWELVE

Tom stood at the table in the Eyrie, packing the bags for New York. He had finished his maths and, although he was not too sure of some of the answers, he had spent an hour on it, and Mr Duncan had said that an hour was quite enough time for anyone to spend on homework. If there was anything he couldn't do in an hour, they would go over it together in school.

At the moment, he was counting out the money they would be taking on the trip to America. Two days earlier they had changed £150 into dollars at the bank, but Tom thought it would not be wise to take it all. Fifty dollars each ought to be enough, he thought, and he put the rest of the money back in the tin they kept on the shelf above his collection of mountain peaks.

As well as the money, he had already packed the two rucksacks with sandwiches, some drinks from the fridge, several guide books, a map and a list of places of interest for them to visit. When Geoff got back from his Saturday morning lesson with Miss Stevenson, they would be crossing the Atlantic again, and this time they would be able to stay a bit longer than half an hour.

Miss Taylor was responsible for several of the items on the list of sights they planned to see. The Deputy Head had found the boys in the library one lunchtime studying a New York guide book, and recommended several places worth visiting if they were ever lucky enough to go there. Apparently she had worked as a dancer on Broadway for a year before going to university. Which was a bit of a surprise. But then life had delivered quite a few surprises recently.

Tom picked up the rucksacks, carried them over to Aquila and was carefully packing them under the seats when his phone rang. It was Geoff, calling to say his lesson was finished and asking if it was all right to tell Aquila to come and pick him up. Tom said it was, stepped back and a moment later the bulk of the life-pod blinked into invisibility. Then, as Tom watched, the faint shimmer in the air outlining its shape disappeared through the window.

Giving instructions to Aquila by phone was a huge improvement on using dog whistles. Now, you simply dialled the number Dunstan had given them and told Aquila what you wanted it to do. You could tell it to come and pick you up, you could send it to pick up someone else and you could even, if you wanted, tell it to take Paige back to Norway and then fly itself back to the water tower. Having the phones meant there would be no more panic about getting lost in New York, nor any risk of getting stuck in a foreign country because someone with a mathematical dog had blown the go-home signal on a whistle.

The phones had been a present from Alan.

'He said he wanted to say thank you for the time you helped him find Dunstan,' Tom's mother had told him when he came home from school to find a box wrapped in silver paper waiting for him on the kitchen table. 'I told him you'd already got a phone, but he said this one's got some extra features you might like.'

The same day, Geoff received an identical parcel, with a note from Alan for Mr and Mrs Reynolds, saying he hoped they wouldn't mind a small gesture of thanks for the help that Geoff had given him.

Later, when Tom and Geoff rang to say thank you, Alan told them he'd been trying to think of a suitable reward for days.

'I asked Dunstan in the end,' he said, 'and he was the one who suggested the phones. I hope he's right and it's what you wanted, but if it's not and you'd prefer something else . . .'

The boys assured him that the phones were exactly what they wanted, and Dunstan had set up the system so they could use them to phone Aquila. They were, he explained, not satellite phones, but used a system that meant they would work in most of the countries around the world. Tom and Geoff could not have been more pleased.

The phones gave them an unexpected bonus as well.

When Aquila reappeared at the water tower, Tom could hear Geoff inside it, asking the lifepod what time it would be in New York when they got there, and Aquila telling him that it would be a little after eight in the morning.

Because Aquila could now talk.

The lifepod's own voice box no longer existed after that photon blast from an Yrrillian battleship six thousand years before, but, as Dunstan explained, it still had the software to convert digital information into sound. The phones gave it the hardware so that it could speak. It had a cheerful, relaxed, rather comforting voice.

'All set?' Geoff asked.

'Everything's packed.' Tom pointed to the rucksacks. 'Food, maps, fifty dollars each . . .'

'Ah . . . we may need a bit more than that,' said Geoff. 'I had a call from Paige this morning. She wants us to get her a top from some shop on Fifth Avenue.'

Tom sighed.

'She says she'll pay us, but she really needs it for a party on Sunday, so if we could fly over with it tomorrow . . .' Geoff grinned sheepishly. 'She says she can get us an invite to the party as well if we like.'

Tom collected the extra dollars from the sweet tin and put them in his pocket. It was still as hard as ever to say no when Paige wanted something done, but he didn't really mind. She, after all, was the reason they had so much money in the first place.

They had been in Norway one afternoon, picnicking on an island off Stavanger, and talking about their next trip to New York. Geoff had been saying how much more fun it would be if they had money to buy something to eat or go to the cinema and Paige had said she couldn't understand why, if they wanted money, they didn't just get a job.

'Because we're not allowed to,' Tom told her. 'We're not old enough.'

Paige waved a hand dismissively, as if this were no excuse. 'Can't you . . . deliver newspapers or something?' She looked at Geoff. 'I mean your dad has a newspaper *shop*, doesn't he?'

It was such a simple idea that the boys couldn't understand why they hadn't thought of it themselves. Delivering newspapers might be bit of a chore if you had to do it on foot, but in Aquila . . .

For nearly a month now, the boys had been doing four paper rounds each morning, and earning a little over seventy pounds a week. With Aquila loaded with newspapers, Geoff would swoop from door to door, hopping over the hedges and walls between the houses, while Tom leaned out the side and pushed the papers through the letter box. They did two paper rounds for Mr Reynolds, two for another newsagent's on the other side of Stavely, and they could finish all of them in a little under fifteen minutes before heading back to the Eyrie to put their feet up and have a second breakfast.

Geoff's father had been particularly impressed. Mr Reynolds said he had never employed anyone as reliable as Tom and Geoff, and what he really admired was the way they never complained about the weather. It didn't matter if it was raining or cold, they just smiled and got on with it. As he told his wife, it was the sort of thing that made you proud to be a father.

'How was it last night?' asked Geoff.

'It was all right.' Tom climbed into Aquila beside his friend. 'If you like that sort of thing.'

The evening before, Alan had taken him, his mother and Dunstan to a theatre in Nottingham to see a production of *A Midsummer Night's Dream*. Tom had never been to a theatre before but on the whole he had enjoyed it. It had certainly made his mother laugh, but he had noticed she did a lot of laughing these days.

'Ready?' asked Geoff.

Tom nodded.

'OK! New York, here we come!' Geoff reached for the controls, but paused before pressing the button that would send them forward. 'A lot's happened since the last time, hasn't it?' he said.

Tom agreed. Since the last time they had crossed the Atlantic, a great deal had happened. Meeting Alan, the business with Paige, Dunstan, getting stuck in Norway . . . All in all the last few weeks had been quite a roller coaster.

And, when he thought about it, Tom couldn't help being struck by how *wrong* he had been a lot of the time. Wrong about Alan, wrong about Dunstan, wrong about Paige . . . Well, not *wrong* exactly . . .

It wasn't that when he'd first met them he'd thought they were one thing and that since then he'd found out they were something else. They were still exactly the sort of people he'd thought they were, it was just that, in the last few weeks, he'd realized they were a lot of other things as well. He'd found they were *more* somehow than he'd realized at the start.

The first time he'd seen Alan, Tom had thought he was one of those men who, if they see something they want in life, simply reach out and take it. And it was true. Alan *was* like that, and one of the things he had wanted and reached out for was Tom's mother. But as the weeks passed Tom had discovered he was other things as well. Alan was someone who had once sat in a classroom and wondered what on earth to do with his life. He was someone who had set up a very successful business despite having no qualifications. He was a dad who cared a good deal about his son, he was generous, he made people laugh, he was frightened of Miss Taylor . . . In fact, he was a whole host of things you could never have guessed from that time Tom had first seen him, sitting in a chair in the living room.

It was the same with Dunstan. Tom had thought when he first met him that Dunstan was one of those slightly odd boys who always seem to be better with computers than they are with people . . . and it was true. Dunstan was very good with computers and not quite so good at conversation. But he was also the most remarkable person Tom had ever met. He had found out about Aquila but said nothing. He had worked out, entirely on his own, how to connect the lifepod to a mobile phone and, on the day that Geoff and Tom were in trouble in Norway, he had come to their rescue. Tom had tried to imagine what it must have been like for an eight-year-old to climb into Aquila and fly across the North Sea on his own . . . and decided that, whatever else he was, Dunstan was also extraordinarily smart and brave.

And then there was Paige. Tom had presumed at the start that she was one of those girls who are only really interested in how they look, and Paige certainly gave a lot of time and attention to her clothes and her hair. But then she was also the only person who had given Tom any sensible advice on how he should cope with Alan. She was the one who had given them the idea of how to use Aquila to get money, and it was Paige – the girl who usually said the first thing that came into her head to anybody – who had kept her promise not to tell anyone about Aquila rather better than Geoff had.

People being more than you thought they were was even true of Miss Taylor. Tom had always thought of the Deputy Head simply as a teacher who made people behave and gave them extra work if they didn't. But Miss Taylor had shown she was much more than that. She was someone who worried if she thought you were overworking, who cared if you were doing enough maths to get to university and who noticed if someone in her class had a talent for running a business but wasn't sure what direction to go in . . .

Was there always more to people than you thought, he wondered? Did they all have bits you didn't notice until you got to know them? Did everyone turn out, like New York, to be even bigger than you'd thought, when you got close?

'You don't mind, do you?' Geoff still hadn't pushed the button that would start them on their journey. 'About going to Norway tomorrow?'

'No,' said Tom. 'No, that's fine.'

'Next weekend,' said Geoff as he eased Aquila up and out through the window, 'you can choose where we go both days, OK? That's a promise. You can go rock collecting anywhere you like.'

'Great,' said Tom.

'Though I do have one suggestion.' Aquila hovered in the air outside the water tower and Geoff pulled back slightly on the handlebars to lift the nose. 'I was thinking the other day that you might find some interesting rocks . . . up there.'

As he spoke, he pointed up to where the round white shape of the moon hung in the clear blue sky directly in front of them.

For a moment, Tom was too astonished to speak.

'I've been talking to Dunstan and he says there's no reason why we shouldn't be able to go there. He says Aquila was designed to do journeys much longer than that. We'd have to check it out, of course. Make sure it was safe, but . . . well, what do you think?'

And Tom thought that like New York, and like the people he was getting to know, their adventure with Aquila just kept on getting bigger.

Turn over to read the first chapter . . .

CHAPTER ONE

It was a Saturday morning and Alex was sitting at the desk in his bedroom, when his father called up to say there was a parcel for him. A parcel sounded interesting, Alex thought, and he hurried downstairs to the kitchen, where his father was studying the label on a box about the size of a small suitcase.

'It's from Godfather John,' he said, as Alex appeared. 'I suppose it's a birthday present.'

Alex's birthday was not for another three months, but presents from Godfather John could arrive at any time in the year, and when they did they were usually . . . unusual.

Last year's present, for instance, had been a Make Your Own Explosions Kit, which Alex still wasn't allowed to play with, and the year before that his godfather had sent a pair of ferrets, with detailed instructions on how to use them to catch rabbits.

'Perhaps we should open it outside,' said Mr Howard doubtfully, remembering the ferrets, but Alex was already tearing off the brown paper and pulling open the lid of the box.

Inside was a battered black case containing a laptop computer.

'Goodness,' said his father. 'How very generous.' He peered into the empty box. 'Is there a card with it? Or a letter?'

Alex was rather disappointed. A laptop computer might sound like an exciting present to get, but this was not, he could see, a new machine. It was old, with spots on it that looked like bits of somebody's lunch. It probably wouldn't be able to do half the things that Alex could do on the computer his parents had given him for Christmas. As presents went, an old laptop was a lot less exciting than a Make Your Own Explosions Kit or a pair of ferrets.

'Are you going to try it out?' asked his father.

'He's not trying out anything till he's done the drying-up.' Alex's mother had appeared in the kitchen, wiping oil and grease off her hands on to a piece of kitchen towel. 'Could someone put the kettle on?'

Ten minutes later, when Alex had finished the drying-up, he took his computer upstairs to his room. It might only be an old laptop, but you never knew. There might be some interesting games on it.

Sitting at his desk, he turned on the machine and a window appeared asking him to type in his name, and then to fill in the date and the time. The date was the fourteenth of May and the clock on his desk said the time was twenty-three minutes past ten, so he tapped in the numbers 10.23.

At least, that was what he meant to do.

In fact he typed in the numbers 10.03.

That wasn't really a problem, though. Alex knew that when you made a mistake on a computer, there was a very simple solution. If you pressed the Control key and then pressed Z, the computer went back to before you had made the mistake.

So that was what he did now.

He pressed Ctrl-Z.

And the computer disappeared.

It took a moment for this to sink in. After all, things *don't* just disappear – especially not computers that you've only had for ten minutes and hardly touched. Alex looked round the room and under the desk – he even looked out of the window, but there was no mistake. The laptop had vanished and there wasn't a sign of it anywhere.

He was still sitting at his desk, wondering what he should do, when his father called up from downstairs to say there was a parcel for him.

Puzzled, Alex went down to the kitchen where he found his father studying the label on a box about the size of a small suitcase.

'It's from Godfather John,' he said when he saw Alex. 'I suppose it's a birthday present.'

Alex stared at the parcel. 'It's the same as the last one!' he said.

'You mean the Make Your Own Explosions Kit?' said his father. 'No, no, that was a much bigger box.' He paused for a moment before adding doubtfully, 'Perhaps we should open it outside.'

Alex stepped forward, tore off the paper and pulled open the lid of the box. Inside was a battered black case, containing a laptop computer.

The whole thing was getting weirder by the second. 'It's another computer,' said Alex. 'Why would he send me another computer?'

'Well, he probably didn't know that we gave you one for Christmas,' said his father, picking a bit of dried egg off the lid. 'And this one's a laptop. Which means you can have it upstairs in your room, if you like. Are you going to try it out?'

'He's not trying out anything till he's done the drying-up.' Alex's mother had appeared in the kitchen, wiping oil and grease off her hands on to a piece of kitchen towel. 'Could someone put the kettle on?'

'I've already done the drying-up,' said Alex. 'I did it just –' he stopped. There on the draining board were all the breakfast dishes. Not more dishes that had been put there since he did the drying-up, but *exactly the same* dishes as before. As if someone had carefully taken them back out of the cupboard, got them wet under a tap and put them out for him to do all over again.

He was beginning to think that the whole world had gone mad – and then he saw the clock.

The clock on the kitchen wall said that the time was eight minutes past ten.

A faint suspicion of what must have happened stirred in his mind. It was quite impossible, of course, and yet . . . and yet . . .

Twelve minutes later, when Alex had finished doing the drying-up for the second time, he was back at his desk in his bedroom with the laptop open in front of him.

After he had turned it on, a window appeared asking him to type in his name, and then to fill in the date and the time. He typed in his name, filled in the date, 14 May, and then the time.

The clock on his desk said the time was twenty-two minutes past ten, but that was not the number he tapped in. Instead, he did exactly what he had done before and carefully tapped in the wrong time – 10.03 – and then pressed the Control key and Z.

The computer disappeared, and Alex sat there, waiting.

He didn't have to wait long.

It was only a minute or so before his father's voice came floating up from downstairs to say there was a parcel for him.

The clock on the kitchen wall said that the time was four minutes past ten. Alex's father was studying the label on a box about the size of a small suitcase and saying, 'It's from Godfather John. I suppose it's a birthday present.'

And then everything happened again. It was the strangest feeling, watching the events unfold – opening the box, finding the computer, his father's surprise, his mother coming in from the garage and saying he had to do the drying-up for the *third* time.

Finally, he was back at his desk in his bedroom, typing his name and address into the computer and then filling in the date and the time . . .

Well, not the time. Not just yet.

Because the time was the secret, he was sure of that. When he typed in 10.03 he had gone back to 10.03, but did that mean if he typed in a different time he would go back to that one instead?

There was only one way to find out.

The clock on the right-hand side of his desk said the time was 10.21. He tapped in 10.20 on the keyboard, then moved the clock from the right-hand side of his desk to the left before pushing down the Control key and tapping the Z.

Instantly, the clock disappeared from the left-hand side of the desk and was back on the right.

And it said the time was 10.20.

He did the same thing again, just to check. This

time, as an experiment, as well as moving the clock from one side of the desk to the other, he moved some books from the shelves by the window to the middle of the floor, and a pair of slippers on to the bed. Sitting back at his desk, the clock said the time was 10.22. He tapped 10.20 into the computer and pressed Ctrl-Z again.

In an instant, the clock had moved back to its original position, the slippers were back under the bed and the books were back on the shelf. Everything was back to exactly how it had been at 10.20.

It was extraordinary. It was the most extraordinary thing that had ever happened to him, Alex thought. It was hard to believe, but it seemed that if you put a time into the computer and pressed Ctrl-Z, you went back to that time.

It was so hard to believe, he thought he had better try it again.

For his next experiment, he decided to make more changes than moving a few books and a pair of slippers. This time, he tipped *all* the books on to the floor, he emptied the entire contents of a box of Lego on to the carpet and then pulled his duvet and pillows off the bed for good measure. While he was pulling the duvet, he knocked his bedside light on to the floor and broke it, and for a moment he wondered how he was going to explain this to his parents. But then he realized he didn't have to explain anything. It didn't *matter* how much damage he did or what he broke because when he pressed Ctrl-Z everything would go back to how it had been before.

He was still standing there thinking about this when his father came in.

'Just wanted to see how you were getting on with –' Mr Howard paused, taking in the bedding on the floor, the Lego scattered on the carpet and the broken bedside light. 'What on earth have you been doing?'

'Ah . . .' said Alex. 'Well . . .'

'You've broken the light,' said his father. 'How did that happen?'

'Um . . .'

'And why's all this stuff on the floor? What's going on?'

Alex was moving towards his desk. 'Hang on a minute,' he said. 'I just have to type in something.'

'You're not typing in anything,' said Mr Howard firmly, 'until you've explained what all this –'

But at that point Alex pressed Ctrl-Z and his father disappeared. Alex was back sitting at his desk, the duvet and pillows were back on the bed and the bedside light was back on the table, unbroken, and the clock said it was twenty minutes past ten.

Looking at the computer screen, he noticed for the first time a little envelope icon in the bottom right-hand corner. When he clicked on it, the menu screen disappeared and was replaced by an email. It said –

Dear Alex

I know you're probably thinking this is a really boring present and you've already got a much better computer, but hold your horses because this machine can do something really quite interesting!

When it asks you to fill in your details, one of the things it'll want you to do is fill in the time. You can always put in the right time, but if you put in an earlier time and press Ctrl-Z, I think the result will surprise you!

Anyway, I hope you have some fun with it and make lots *of mistakes!*

Your loving godfather

John Presley

PS It might be best not to mention any of this to your parents. They'd probably just take it away like they did the Explosions Kit!

Alex read the email through twice. He had no idea why Godfather John should want him to make lots of mistakes, but that was only one of several questions buzzing round his brain. Like where the laptop had come from, who had made it, and how it worked . . .

The door opened and his father came in.

'Just wanted to see how you were getting on with your birthday present,' he said. 'Does it work?'

'Yes, yes, it does,' said Alex. He stood up. 'I thought I might take it round and show Callum.'

'Won't he be busy this morning,' said Mr Howard, 'with the party?'

'That's not till this afternoon,' said Alex. He closed the lid of the laptop. 'And there's a program on here I think he'd like to see.'

He had a feeling that his friend Callum would be particularly interested in Ctrl-Z.

It all started with a Scarecrow

Puffin is well over sixty years old.
Sounds ancient, doesn't it? But Puffin has never been
so lively. We're always on the lookout for the next big
idea, which is how it began all those years ago.

Penguin Books was a big idea from the mind of
a man called Allen Lane, who in 1935 invented
the quality paperback and changed the world.
**And from great Penguins, great Puffins grew,
changing the face of children's books forever.**

The first four Puffin Picture Books were hatched in 1940 and the
first Puffin story book featured a man with broomstick arms called
Worzel Gummidge. In 1967 Kaye Webb, Puffin Editor, started the
Puffin Club, promising to **'make children into readers'**.
She kept that promise and over 200,000 children became
devoted Puffineers through their quarterly instalments of
Puffin Post, which is now back for a new generation.

Many years from now, we hope you'll look back and
remember Puffin with a smile. **No matter what your age
or what you're into, there's a Puffin for everyone.**
The possibilities are endless, but one thing is for sure:
whether it's a picture book or a paperback, a sticker book
or a hardback, **if it's got that little Puffin
on it – it's bound to be good.**